FORBIDDEN LUST

ELITE MEN OF MANHATTAN BOOK 1

MISSY WALKER

D1666823

Cover Design: Missy Walker

Editor: Swish Design & Editing

For Jen, my sister from a different mister

PREFACE

Dolls are precious
Perfect in appearance
Flawless
But over time dolls crack
Fracturing their very existence
Breaking their flawless façade

1

LOURDE

I had the name of a porn star—Lourde Diamond—seriously, Mom and Dad, thanks a lot.

The only difference between me and said porn star was my bank balance.

We were wealthy. Well, my family was rich—old money. My dad, like his daddy and his daddy before him, were media moguls, owning the greatest media empire in North America. Their wives were hand-picked from noteworthy families and perfectly curated—primed, aristocratic, well-mannered, and relentless in playing their part and owning their duty. At eighteen, that's where my life was headed. It was abundantly clear by dearest Momma, being the perfect wife was an achievement one must uphold. Since maids helped me learn to walk, they had groomed me for the day when it would be my turn to become a wife. Etiquette, posture, finishing school, every other class, you name it, I'd done it.

Perfect in every part. I was waiting to be introduced to the perfect partner from a prestigious family, of course. Old money, preferably, as Momma would say. Did I tell you it was the twenty-first century? Fuck, you'd be correct for thinking we were in the fifties. You'd also be right in assuming I was getting bored with my life, bored with being prim and proper and what society expected of me.

After I slid the white satin glove down my forearm, then the next, I rested them on the ivory tulle of my balloon skirt. Next, I slid the tray of canapes closer. Popping one into my mouth, I swallowed the buttery salmon with horseradish cream on a thin wafer. Then picked up another, my tummy growling satisfactorily at the intake of food.

With my best friends, Pepper and Grace, I'd just finished my debutante ball. It was by invitation extended to high-society Manhattan, a tradition my mother wanted to uphold, regardless of my months of objections. *Who wants to celebrate the coming out of a young girl into a woman?*

News flash—I'd become a woman a few months ago when Josh took my V-card.

Now we were back at the sprawling penthouse on Park Avenue where I live with my parents, celebrating with a sprinkle of friends, but mostly Daddy's esteemed guests. I popped another canape in my mouth and glanced around. This wasn't a party for me, more like a gathering of Dad and Mom's favorite people.

With his perfectly groomed salt-and-pepper hair and tuxedo, Dad stood chatting with my boyfriend, Josh, and his parents. Josh, or Joshua, as Dad called him, is my boyfriend of three months. Introduced by our parents, Josh studied law at Cambridge and was following his parents' footsteps, who owned one of the oldest and prestigious law firms in Manhattan.

To the left, there was Momma, not a hair out of place with some other ladies of class in the Manhattan social circle. Next to her was my brother, Connor. He was conversing with his best friends, Barrett, Ari, and Magnus. With eight years between Connor and me, I wondered why they even had me at all. We looked nothing alike. I took after Dad with porcelain skin, hazel eyes, light brown hair, and high cheekbones, whereas Connor had Mom's striking blue eyes and blonde hair. The only thing we had in common was our height.

Connor looked over and raised his glass of champagne. I smiled. Then Barrett turned toward me and ever so slightly tipped his mouth into a smile. His stare from across the room pulled my breath into my throat.

I can't help it.

I still had a stupid crush on Barrett. Green eyes and dark brown almost black hair. He wasn't a boy. He was a man with broad shoulders, golden-colored muscles, and confidence in spades. A completely off-limits older man with fuck-all interest in his best friend's baby sister.

Barrett helped broker a deal for a brownstone in Brooklyn for my family. But Connor struck a friendship with Barrett, encouraging Barrett to go out and establish his own construction and development company—just completing his first boutique hotel renovation in Soho.

So what if I made a point to search social media to see who was on his arm this week. I wasn't a creep. Just curious was all. The man was like a vault. I knew this because my parents regularly invited him over for dinner when Connor came around, yet he was the most mysterious man ever.

"There you are," Josh said, pulling me away from my stupid one-sided crush. Instantly, guilt washed over me.

"Here I am." I smiled up at him, then grabbed another canape.

"Have you eaten all these?" He laughed, then pushed the tray away from me and toward the middle of the table.

Quickly, I glanced back at Barrett, but he was engrossed in conversation with the boys.

Ugh.

"I wish we could go now. This party is lame. I don't even get the whole debutante thing. I'm coming out to society. Where was I before?"

He raised a brow. "Don't be like that. It's tradition. Also, an excellent opportunity to meet people and network."

I don't need to network.

Josh looked past me and smiled at a man who slowed down near us.

"Senator, how nice to see you here," Josh said.

"Joshua, what are you doing here?"

"This is my girlfriend, Lourde Diamond."

God, it sounded worse than *Debbie Does Dallas.*

"Senator Masele, nice to see you again." I stood up and greeted him.

"Lourde, hello, dear, and congratulations on making your debut."

I smiled and nodded.

"Of course, you two would know each other." Josh smiled, and I noticed his jaw tick.

"I didn't know you two were dating. What a match made in society heaven. Your mother must be thrilled, Lourde."

"Ecstatic." I smiled sweetly.

He looked at me sideways, unsure if my answer was caked in sarcasm. It was.

After another boring hour of networking—as Josh aptly named it—we had arrived downtown. Seated in a private section of a club, Pepper and Grace sat beside me, sipping on bubbles, while Connor and Barrett sat opposite with dates who appeared like magnets when we arrived.

"This is so much better. Thanks for organizing, Connor," I said above the booming bass.

He took his attention from the woman whispering something in his ear. "No problem, sis, it's a big day for you."

I smiled, my gaze settling on Barrett and his date. I wish they weren't here—the women—that is. But if I had my boyfriend here, what was the big deal if they had company?

I looked around the club. *Where was Josh exactly?*

"So, what are your plans now? You're a woman and all." The way the word 'woman' rolled off Barrett's tongue made my thighs clench together.

Stop it, Lourde.

Your boyfriend was probably hurling over the toilet from the bottle of champagne he downed, and you're drooling over your silly man-crush.

I pushed away my wavy hair. "I'm thinking about helping with the family business."

Barrett smiled, and fuck, there went my ovaries. At the same time, my brother choked on his whiskey, and reluctantly, I peeled my eyes away from Barrett. The Ms. Universe lookalike seated next to him rubbed him on the back, soft enough to do absolutely nothing. He didn't thank her. Instead, he looked up at me. "Since when, sis?"

"I've been thinking about it for a while. Maybe I could be an editor for a design magazine?"

He rolled his eyes. "None of the women in the Diamond family have ever worked, Lourde, and it's not starting now."

Barrett turned to my brother, arching a dark brow, but he said nothing. If he was surprised, he didn't voice it.

Walls felt as though they were closing in around my chest. "We're not in 1950 anymore!"

Pepper and Grace stopped their conversation and turned toward me.

"Sis," Connor said.

"Maybe we should dance?" Pepper squeezed my hand from under the table.

"Yes!" Grace had already shuffled out of the booth before I'd responded. Deciding I was sick of this discussion, I slid out after Pepper.

I swayed my hips on the dance floor. Then, sliding my hands down my ruby red dress that gripped my body, I closed my eyes and let the beat overcome me. Or perhaps it was the two glasses of bubbles I quickly downed. Whatever, I didn't care. I felt free.

After a while, I opened my eyes, my gaze settling on our table. Barrett's green eyes stared back at me. My cheeks burned cherry red while my skin heated all over. Thank God it was dark.

"Hey, where's Josh?"

I blinked a few times, then turned to Grace, who was looking at me curiously.

"B… bathroom," I managed to get out, and when I glanced back at Barrett, his lady friend had her hands around his neck.

Did I just imagine the whole thing? Ugh.

"Actually, I might check," I said to the girls who were dancing to "Unapologetic Bitch" by Madonna. Josh had said he was going to the toilet but had been gone for a while.

On the way to the bathroom, I bumped into Magnus and asked if he could check if Josh was, in fact, keeled over in the men's bathroom. After he came out, he informed me Josh wasn't there.

What the hell. I didn't know at this point if I was more aggravated over my brother's sexist comment, Barret for giving me that spine-tingling stare, or my missing boyfriend. And tonight was meant to be about me?

Finally, I gave up scouring the crowd and slipped out the back exit in need of some quiet. Outside, the air was brutally cold—the wind whipping down the sidewalk, tossing my hair around my shoulders. The music lowered to a dull thud, giving me the space to hear my own thoughts. Moans pulled my attention, and curiously I walked toward the sound.

I turned the corner.

No.

A girl with a tacky pleather skirt and a blonde bob was on her knees with Josh's dick in her mouth. "What the fuck, Josh?"

His eyes enlarged to the size of saucepans. "Oh, shit." He tried to zip up and push her aside, but I was already running away. I turned the corner and ran back toward the club. Nearly tripping over, I slammed into a chest and a scent so intoxicating, it momentarily pulled me away from my existence.

"Lourde?"

I stared up into his green eyes. It was Barrett, and I couldn't help it. My eyes spilled with tears.

"What happened? Do you want me to get your brother?" he asked.

I glared at him, fuming at the idea.

"Okay, not Connor. Just tell me what happened."

"I just saw my boyfriend getting a blow job in the alleyway."

"What the fuck?" His eyes darkened with rage. "I'll kill him," he said, his tone like ice.

"No, just take me home." I stared up at him, pleading.

He balled his fists by his sides.

"Please, Barrett." My voice came out on the verge of begging.

He put his arm around me, and we quickly walked in the opposite direction toward his car. In under ten minutes, we were back in front of 147 Park Avenue. Moments later, after sitting in silence, he turned to me.

"Hey, you okay?"

I kept my gaze down. I didn't want him to see my tear-stained cheeks and smeared mascara eyes. His fingers wrapped around my chin, tilting my face so I'd have no option but to face him.

"Don't think twice about him. You deserve so much better than that asshole."

His hands lingered on my chin, his thumb stroking my cheek.

"Of course, you're going to say that."

"What, why?" He removed his hand, but the warmth of his touch remained.

"You're just being kind. It's what everyone says to comfort someone. But what I really want to know is, why? What did I do to deserve *that?*"

"Nothing, you did absolutely nothing."

Sobs clogged my throat.

"Come here, Lourde."

He unclipped my seat belt, and with one deft move, lifted me over the center console and onto his lap, pulling me into his chest. Firm, broad muscles were everywhere, and his scent was a cocktail of manly things like tobacco, whiskey, and something forbidden.

When I wrapped my arms around his neck, his hands dipped lower around my waist. The air in the car grew thick. He was all I needed to forget. I glanced up, and his hooded eyes stared back. My heart thundered in my chest. "Will you make me forget?" I whisper.

I moved slightly closer, but he made no move to kiss me. Instead, he looked away and slid his hands from around my waist. "Lourde," he said, his voice like gravel.

"Just forget it, Barrett." I pulled the door latch open, stepped out as quickly as possible without splitting a side seam, and ran toward the glowing double doorways.

Fuck my life.

2

LOURDE

Five years later.

"Tell me again why we didn't fly?" My boyfriend, Hunter Polmeo, the third asked of anyone who'd listen.

We were on the busy road driving to the Hamptons. Rows of cars on the I-495 sat idling like statues under the glaring midday heat. Inside his Porsche Cayenne, I sat next to Pepper and her boyfriend, Jake, who were good friends with Hunter. Grace was with her boyfriend, Dane, in the Audi behind us with two more of Hunter's single friends.

"Fuck knows, brother," Jake spat out. "Hopefully, it won't be long."

"Are you kidding? Day one of summer, and we're packed in here with the riff-raff," Hunter said, a scowl plastered across his face.

"We'll get there, Hunter. Just chill." I rolled my eyes at Pepper, feeling a headache coming on. Although, he was probably right. We were at a standstill with no movement in sight.

Three hours after leaving Manhattan, we'd finally arrived. My headache had kicked in and was now a thundering migraine. So instead of unpacking, I laid down, hoping it would be better by tonight, and I could enjoy the party.

When I woke up from a brief nap, although better, I still didn't feel up to going out. Walking out of the bedroom I was sharing with Hunter, I made my way toward the laughter in the living room. Pepper sat on the charcoal couch next to Grace, who had her hands wrapped around Dane's neck as she sat on his lap.

Jake, was with Hunter, pouring shots of something clear on the deck while Sebastian and Kyle, who were tagging along for the summer, sucked down their shots in record time, then slammed their glasses down for refills. *Ugh.* I wondered if Hunter was just serving or consuming. He promised me he wouldn't drink today, especially since he had gotten blind drunk last night.

"Lourde, how's your headache?" Pepper asked, coming around to hug me

"Still there." I squeezed her, then let go, stepping back to admire her outfit. "You look hot!" She wore her recent purchase from Saks—a purple sweetheart dress. Her long jet-black hair fell around her shoulders, her olive skin a nod to her Greek heritage.

She twirled. "I know, I love it!"

"Here she is!" Grace hopped off Dane's lap and walked toward me. Strikingly opposite of Pepper, her curly copper hair, freckles, and green eyes popped against the white pants suit and stilettos she donned.

Hunter turned and headed inside after spotting me. He stepped behind me, wrapping his arms around my waist.

"You like, hun?" he asked, gesturing toward the view that lay beyond the floor-to-ceiling glass windows.

"Yes, it's nice." Clean lines and sharp edges filled the newly built residence he had rented in East Hampton. It wasn't my style. I preferred the character-filled older homes, but the view was stunning.

"It's nice?" He blew out, and the fruity agave scent of tequila escaped him, so too did his promise of an alcohol-free night. He dropped his hands and stepped in front of me, annoyance flickering behind his eyes.

I smiled. "It's a stunner, Hunter," I said, stroking his ego. If I learned anything about him over the last year of our dating, it was his need for gratification and praise.

His family came from a long line of senators and politicians, and he had a lot of weight on his shoulders. We were introduced during the Diamond's annual charity ball. By chance? Absolutely not. Everything in my life was planned out with precision, leaving no room for chance.

But Hunter was a nice guy, good-looking, and apart from his foul temper, he treated me well. But we both were aware of the not-so-subtle arrangement in place for the two of us. I tried to ignore the pressure mounting on me, but it was difficult. We were both twenty-three, in the prime of our lives, with the expectation to marry, settle down, and have children.

I shook my head. That's why this trip to the Hamptons was a trip I was counting on. Let my hair down with my best friends and just spend time with my boyfriend without the pressure that surrounded us. In the meantime, I just needed this migraine to subside and for him to take a chill pill.

He narrowed his eyes. "Jesus, fuck, just once try to seem pleased, Lourde."

Geez. It was all I could do not to roll my eyes.

"What?" I threw my hands up in the air, but he'd already turned and headed for the balcony.

We were here! Why couldn't he just be happy for once instead of the moody guy he's turned into?

Momma had pulled me aside last month, hinting a proposal wasn't far away. We certainly hadn't started on the right foot if a proposal was on the cards these holidays. The thought scared me, and I pushed it away from my mind. Whether to him or anyone else my parents introduced me to, a proposal was just a metal box and a cage for another Diamond woman. Unfortunately, I knew it was coming, and there wasn't a damn thing I could do about it. Over the years, I'd accepted my role and slowly given up on having any dreams of my own. It didn't mean I had to like it, though.

Pepper left Jake's side and appeared by mine. We watched as they both walked outside. "What was that all about?" she asked.

"Hunter just being Hunter," I said, shrugging it off. He wasn't a fan of long drives and could get rather irritable.

"Oh, I know, and there you go defending him again," she said, popping her dark eyes.

Pepper had witnessed Hunter's temper. It certainly wasn't the first time he'd made a display in front of my friends. Sometimes, I wondered if he liked the attention. But whatever. I had an elephant trespassing between my temples, and I wasn't in the mood to argue. Plus, any minute, they'd be heading to Montauk to the party to kick off the season.

"So, you sure you want to stay here, hun?" Pepper asked, placing a hand on my shoulder.

"I need to sleep this off. Otherwise, I have zero chance of making it out later to meet you guys."

"Okay, well, sleep, and then hopefully, you can meet up with us later."

I nodded, watching Hunter laugh with his two single friends, completely oblivious to the fact he'd hurt my feelings.

Dressed in black pants and a tight white shirt that showed off his muscles, I wondered if Hunter was really going to propose this summer. Goosebumps sprang up on my forearms, my arms crossing automatically around my waist.

My gaze remained on him, but as I imagined him on bended knee, another image flooded into view. Green eyes, brown almost black hair, taller than your average man, thickly built with a hint of a five o'clock shadow. The silhouette of Barrett appeared at the forefront of my mind. I twisted my lips, smiling at the thought. One day it would be him who looked at me across the table at dinner with those mysterious eyes.

Keep dreaming, Lourde.

Quickly, I shook away the feeling. *Stupid crush.* It wasn't like I could avoid Barrett, though he was at the house nearly every week for dinner with Connor.

A hand circled my waist, and I jerked. "It's just me. You look like you're miles away, babe."

I looked down, recognizing the black ring on Hunter's pinky finger and swallowed down the guilt. "I'm just unwell, that's all."

"I'm sorry about what happened before, hun. But you know how I can get sometimes. It was a long drive."

"Of course, don't sweat it," I said, surprised by his apology.

"Uber's here," Dane and Grace both yelled, then smiled at each other. I rolled my eyes. They were so in love they even thought the same.

Hunter gave me a chaste kiss on the mouth before pinching my ass. "Sleep it off, hun, and maybe you can make it up to me later." He winked. The taste of tequila and cigarettes lingered on my lips.

Pepper and Grace took turns hugging me.

"Girls… come… on!" Hunter's voice was curt as he stopped on the stairs that led from the deck down to the street.

"Go," I said. The last thing I wanted was to set off his mood.

"We're coming," Grace yelled back and ran back in her stilettos.

"Call me if you need me," Pepper said, feeling my forehead.

"No temp," I said. "Just a hammer in my head."

"Okay, go to bed. I've got my phone," Pepper said, grabbing her phone out of her Chanel bag, then swiping.

Pepper's parents and my parents had been friends since we were little. Pepper and I instantly hit it off. We both liked the same things—parties, shoes, and *Sex and the City*. Okay, maybe we were slightly obsessed with *Sex and the City*. Were re-runs still called re-runs if you watched them hundreds of times?

"Battery's running low. Damn, I forgot to charge it." A frown fell across her dark features.

"It's all good. Hunter will have his." I waved my hand in the air, trying to usher her out. "Go. Have fun."

Three hours later, two Tylenol and nearly a gallon of water, my throbbing headache had completely disap-peared. In record time, I'd showered, washed, and dried my hair and chose the perfect outfit for day one of my summer vacation in the Hamptons. Not bad.

Dark brown eyes accented by swipes of mascara through my lashes and pale pink lips completed the look with my teal green satin dress with a high slit and recent shoe purchase of strappy pale nude heels. I stared at myself in the mirror.

My voluminous sun-streaked, wavy hair fell to my mid-back as I pulled one half over with a nude suede clip.

"Hunter won't know what hit him," I said aloud.

3

BARRETT

I was the quiet one in the group. It wasn't too hard when your mates were all so fucking loud. I noticed the bar patrons on the sky deck terrace shooting us daggers, then promptly turned around when evidently one of them recognized us, likely Connor.

He was all over the news, having just broken up with a Victoria's Secret model, and if that wasn't publicity enough, Connor was the Vice President of Diamond Incorporated—the largest media company in North America.

Years ago, Connor introduced me to Ari and Magnus, and the four of us had been tight since, bonding over our love of whiskey and craft beers, gorgeous women, and zero fucks about anyone else. Oh, and money, of course, we loved money. Ari's grandmother owned an international fashion label, and Magnus' family recently floated their third-generation tech company.

Unlike my friends, I didn't have a trust fund I could fall back on. I had to make my own money, and fuck, I made it. The skyscraper we were sitting in, sipping on our ice-cold craft beers imported from Australia, I built.

Well, ZF Constructions, the company I owned, did. And yeah, if you're wondering, ZF stands for Zero Fucks. But that isn't public knowledge, unlike my bank account balance *Forbes* divulged last year. *Fuckers.*

Now every gold-digging woman in Manhattan wanted my cock. Not that they didn't before. Pussy was easy. Too fucking easy. Women fell into two categories—gold diggers and women who wanted a relationship, sinking their claws into me and never letting go. I wanted neither. Convenient fucks were where I drew the line.

"Barrett, you did well," Connor said, holding up his glass and clinking it with mine. Ari and Magnus followed, clinking their craft beers with me as we sat around the oak table on the skydeck overlooking Central Park.

"Thanks, I have a great team."

"Always so modest." Ari slapped me between the shoulder blades.

"Yeah, man, you should be proud of all this. It's remarkable," Magnus added, wide-eyed as he took in the finishes and clientele.

Proud? I could never be proud of myself. Not if I built a thousand towers this grand. I didn't deserve happiness of any kind.

My gaze followed Magnus and settled where round tables and chairs surrounded the curved marble bar. Wooden feature walls and soft furnishings softened sleek lines. I couldn't lay claim to the design. My interior designer had an eye for detail and an edge that made us shine. That's why I headhunted her from the competition. When I wanted something, I got it, whether it was staff or an award-winning tower. This skyscraper we built was a masterpiece. Celebrities and billionaires all wanted a residence at 21 Park, with the tower selling out before construction had even begun.

"It was Olivia who designed it," I added.

"Olivia? Is that the one with the blonde bob who has inflatable lips I'd like to wrap around my—"

"Shut the fuck up, Magnus," I snapped before he could finish.

He tilted his head. "Come on. You can't tell me you haven't thought about it. You've slept with half of Manhattan, for fuck's sake."

I narrowed my eyes, shaking my head. "I don't shit where I eat."

"I'd eat Oli—"

"Magnus, we get it. You'd eat her out if you could. I wonder how Leila feels about that. You know, your wife?" Ari questioned him, drinking the rest of his pale ale.

"My wife has cock up to her ears," Magnus said, a slight twitch in his jaw. "Anyway, when's the last time you got laid, Ari, or are you liking cock more these days?"

Ari abruptly pushed out his chair. "What the fuck, Magnus?"

Not that I made it a habit to know when my friends hooked up, but I couldn't remember the last time I saw Ari with a woman.

"Fellas, chill," Connor said.

"I'm more chill than a fucking cucumber," Ari said.

I shot Magnus daggers. Puffy circles surrounded his eyes, and lines formed around the edges of his mouth. I knew little about married life, but shit, if you looked like that after being married three months, why do it?

"So you keeping this one too?" Ari asked, waving his hand around, referring to the skyscraper we were in. I'd built and kept several boutique hotels and smaller commercial buildings, but 21 Park was my biggest deal yet, and I sold her. Today.

"No. The deal's done," I said, gulping my beer. "How is Leila, Magnus?" I asked as he stared at the big-breasted waitress coming our way. Throwing him a bit more shade wouldn't hurt.

"A man can look, can't they? Leila certainly does." He shrugged, his eyes not leaving the woman.

"What? Wait. You sold 21 Park?" Connor asked, slamming down his glass on the table.

Magnus, Ari, and Connor stared at me. I nodded, swiping a hand through my dark hair.

"What the hell, Barrett? We just cheered you for finishing 21 Park!" Ari said in confusion.

"To who?" Magnus asked as three sets of eyes stared at me like I had two heads.

"Russian billionaire, Nikolay Petrov. It will be in the *Times* tomorrow. I thought by now, someone would've probably leaked it."

"No, Mr. Fucking Mysterious," Connor said, visibly irritated. "This is a huge deal, Barrett. Why didn't you tell us?"

I shrugged. Maybe I ought to have told the boys, but I didn't see what difference it made to them if I did.

"Did you make a pretty penny?" Ari asked.

"Nearly doubled my in." A smirk spread across my cheeks.

"Jesus, fuck." Connor drank two fingers of his freshly poured glass of whiskey.

"Good on you, bud." Ari slapped me between the shoulder blades. "You work hard enough."

"Thanks."

"What can I get you, boys?" The waitress appeared

with her brown hair and popping hazel eyes. Lourde's face instantly came to the forefront of my mind. I shook my head, removing the thought. She was still Connor's much younger sister and completely off-limits. Too bad she'd grown into a buxom beauty, and her choice of men were all fuckwits. Just last week, she bent over in front of me at the weekly dinner her family always invited me to. I was only human as I imagined plowing into her perfect apple of an ass.

"I could eat the entire left side of the menu," Connor said. His voice clawed me back to reality.

Okay, so maybe there were a few times where I was banging the latest model and wishing it was the back of Lourde Diamond. We all had fantasies. And I saw the way she looked at me too. She wanted to fuck me. It wasn't just one-sided, dammit. It would be a hell of a lot easier if it were. Her debutante ball was where I saw her at her most vulnerable. She looked at me with eyes I could barely say no to. But I did. I had to.

I'm sure she hated me more than…

"Barrett?" I turned to Magnus, who was waiting for me for fuck knows what.

"What's that?"

The waitress was looking at me with her iPad in hand.

"We've all ordered. What do you want?" Magnus questioned.

"Nothing. I've got to jet. I'm going to the Hamptons tonight."

"What now?" He flicked his wrist, staring down at his shiny gold Rolex. "It's nearly ten o'clock at night?"

"I'm taking the chopper."

"Oh," the waitress cooed, dragging her eyes up and down, then settled her gaze upon me.

Another time, gorgeous.

"We're hungry, sweetheart. Don't you have to put our order in?" Magnus asked, giving her a wave.

The waitress scowled before turning on her heel toward the open kitchen.

"You know Lourde is in the Hamptons with her boyfriend. I think she's there for the summer."

"Is she?" I said evenly.

Connor regarded me. "Uh-huh."

"Need me to check up on her?" I half-joked.

"Yeah, maybe. The guy she's with, Hunter, I'm still deciding on, although Mom loves him."

"Hunter, the third," I said.

Ever since I've known Connor, he'd always been hard on his little sister. Actually, his entire family has held the strings that control her every move her entire life—playing puppet master, controlling whom she dates, not allowing her to work in the family business. At one time, I thought Lourde would stand up to them, but now I think she's so used to the Diamond way, she's lost her way.

"So, you remember him? He was at the dinner a few months ago."

I nodded. "I always remember a name." How could I not? The guy was young, good-looking, and had his paws all over Lourde. But there was something about him that got under my skin. "I got you, Connor. I'll keep an eye out," I said.

We hadn't officially had *the* talk, but Connor made it abundantly clear she was totally off-limits to any of his friends. We were all assholes anyway, and Lourde was a princess, better than all of us. But a simple fuck would get her out of my mind for good. I was sure of it.

Dream on.

"You know she's meant to marry this guy?" Connor asked.

"What?" I nearly choked on my beer.

"You all right?"

"Fine."

"Sure about that?" Magnus smiled at me. *What was his deal tonight?*

"Mom and Dad set her up with Hunter the third. It turned out perfectly, seeing they actually liked each other, and with Hunter's dad next in line to be the Governor of New York, it's perfect for both families."

"Right." My collar itched around my neck, so I pulled on it, loosening it. "And she knows this?"

"She understands. It's not like we hide anything. There are certain responsibilities that come with carrying the Diamond name."

"God, it's so much easier to come from nothing and work your way up."

"Is it?" Connor looked at me with an expression I hadn't seen before. My body coiled like it did that night. Her body in my arms, lifeless and lying in a pool of blood. I kept my past to myself. All they knew was I had a sister, and my parents died in a car accident. The last part was a lie.

"Do you remember those summers in the Hamptons, the four of us? The women, the parties?" Magnus asked, pulling me from my nightmare.

"You make out like we're sixty the way you're talking instead of just curling past thirty," Ari said, sitting back down.

"Yeah, we were there last year, all except the married man." We all glared at Magnus.

"She made me go to St Bart's. What could I do?" He held his hands up.

Connor stared down at Magnus' groin.

"What the fuck are you doing?" Magnus asked.

23

"I'm just seeing if you have any balls left or if Leila has them tucked away in her Chanel clutch."

We all laughed.

"Just wait, fellas, till you're married. You'll see what I mean."

"God, help me when that day comes," Connor added, hanging his head low.

"Not me. I'm getting sick of fucking around, but Jesus, it's hard to find anyone decent in this town," Ari said.

"Anyone else notice Barrett's silence on this one?" Ari asked. Connor and Magnus glared at me.

I slid my wallet and keys into my Armani pants. "Sorry, just thinking about the leggy blonde that's going to be riding me till sunrise when I get to my house in Montauk."

"Lucky fucker," Magnus mumbled. The other guys chuckled and cheered.

"How long are you there for?" Connor asked.

"I've got something brewing with a site in East Hampton, so could be days, could be weeks."

"Maybe if I can escape, I'll join you," he said.

"Did I hear a trip coming up?" Magnus and Ari's ears pricked up.

"I don't know if I can, boys. We're an editor down, and I'm pulling more slack," Connor added.

"Well, give me a yell if you boys want to catch up." I stood, my chair gliding back on the wood floor.

"Seriously, man, congrats on the sale. I know you don't like the praise, but you did well," Connor said, and he meant it.

"Thanks, bud."

I waved goodbye and disappeared down the ninety floors to the busy Manhattan streets to my waiting car.

"The helipad, Billy," I said as he closed the door behind me.

Maybe the Hamptons wouldn't be such a drag if I checked in on Lourde and her cocky boyfriend. A smile pulled from the edges of my mouth.

4

LOURDE

The party was in full swing by the time I arrived. Women wore their latest designs fresh off the catwalk and paraded around the home, dancing and grinding against the men who allowed them. And they all let them. The house belonged to actress, Jennifer Jones. Hunter's aunt knew her, and that's how he scored an invitation. I didn't dare mention I had Jen's cell number, Hunter jealousy would reach a new level, had I said that. Over the years, Jen, with her philanthropy work, had hosted the annual Diamond charity ball, and we'd enjoyed dinner a handful of times when she was on the East Coast rather than her hometown of Los Feliz.

In the living area, a band played jazz fusion. It had me swaying and loosening up as I continued to meander throughout the expansive home, soaking in the laid-back atmosphere and hypnotic music. Polished concrete floors with wallpapered walls and angular ceilings led out to the pool, where I spotted Pepper and Jake.

Taking a glass of champagne that was offered to me by

the waiter, I set off toward Pepper and Jake. Shimmying past laughing, carefree partygoers, I took a large gulp, hoping it would make me loosen up and unwind. Day one of the summer… *give it time, Lourde.*

"Lourde!" Pepper wrapped her arms around me, then stepped back.

"Wowsers, you look ravishing," she said, staring at the slit of my dress.

"Why, thank you." I smiled. "Think Hunter will agree?"

"Heck, yes." Jake grinned, throwing me a wink.

I laughed.

"Eyes on the prize, Jakey boy." Pepper grabbed his chin and tilted it toward her, then sat back down on his lap.

I knew she was joking. Pepper wasn't the type to get jealous. She and Jake were more solid than a Manhattan prenup. "Only eyes for you, baby," he purred, wrapping his hands around her ass and planting kisses up her neck.

Pepper giggled.

"Get a room!" I blew out, wishing Hunter was that affectionate with me.

Pepper side-glanced at me and winked. "So, have you caught up with him?"

"Who, Hunter?" I slid down next to them on the sunken outdoor lounge.

"I've gone from the front to the back of the home and can't find Hunter or Grace and the others."

"They were upstairs a while back," Jake said. "Some people from the party have also moved on down to the beach."

I peered over the glass balcony toward the endless sand, where bodies appeared like moving shadows in the distance. The dark gray-black ocean crashed and roared under the amber moonlight. The harmonic wave of a saxophone sounded against the ocean, and the sweet sound mixed with the champagne had my body humming.

"Another champagne, miss?"

"Please." The waiter handed me the tall glass of bubbles, then one for Pepper.

"Headache's gone?" Pulling me from the abyss, I turned toward Pepper.

Smiling, then taking a large sip, I said, "I'm a new girl."

"Amazing." Pepper grinned.

"How amazing is this summer going to be?" Jake pulled Pepper in for a kiss.

The two of them were too cute, but tonight I wasn't about to be the third wheel. I stood up, smoothing down the satin of my dress.

"Can't wait." I smiled at the two lovebirds, slightly resentful I didn't have that kind of relationship with Hunter. "I'll catch up with you guys soon, just going to find Hunter."

Clutching my champagne, I headed to the top floor via the external spiral staircase.

Whoa. What a view. East Hampton was home to some gorgeous homes, but Jennifer Jones' house was something else. Hopefully, I'd bump into her soon. From up here, views stretched all the way toward the lighthouse and across the sandy dunes to Montauk.

"Hey." A smooth voice made me turn around.

Hunter's friend appeared decidedly intoxicated with bloodshot eyes. "Sebastian! Have you seen Hunter?"

He laughed before mumbling something I couldn't quite make out.

"You look like a tall glass of whiskey." He stepped in closer, his eyes dragging down my body. God, he smelled like a brewery. The last thing I needed was for Hunter to witness Sebastian hitting on me. He'd undoubtedly split his face open and ruin the summer for the rest of us.

I stepped back. "Hey, thanks. I'm just looking for Hunter. Have you seen him?"

He pointed down toward the beach. "They went down there."

That would explain why I couldn't find Grace and Dane, either. They must have started their own party on the dunes.

"You deserve so much better than him." He breathed out, placing his hand on my bare shoulder.

"Hey, do you need me to call you an Uber?" I asked, patting his hand away with his wayward drunken comment.

"Always the perfect one, Lourde. Have you ever once colored outside the lines?"

I blinked, trying to register his seemingly coherent question. "What lines?"

"I dare you to defy your last name and have some real fun."

I stared at him, and something within me stirred.

He shook his head before I could reply. "Go on, find your man," he said. I watched him leave and unsteadily navigate the spiral staircase.

Color outside the lines. That didn't exist for a girl like me when my life was monochrome. Plus, the lines were more like large Manhattan blocks. Large enough to keep me happy... *for now.* I pushed the thought away and, after a brief search upstairs that turned up empty, I descended the staircase toward the private pathway to the beach.

Summer was here. If the lines were claustrophobic, I wouldn't have any sense of them now. I was away from

Manhattan and my controlling mother and brother whose arguments with Dad had reached a new high.

I kicked off my heels as soon as my feet hit the sand. It squeaked cool between my manicured toes. The salty, warm air blew my wavy hair off my face, and each step I took, my foot kicked up sand around my ankles. The ocean roared and dragged back the sand. I took in the small group of people gathered along the dune, but none of their faces were Hunter or Grace.

Ugh. I gathered my dress up and held it so it didn't get ruined.

Maybe he doubled back to the house to check on me.

I shook my head.

Walking some more, I noticed another group ahead.

Strange noises pricked at my ears. *What was that?* Seriously suspect moaning and groaning noises caught the wind and traveled in my direction. The last thing I needed to witness were strangers getting it on, but I needed to pass. A large group was further ahead, and I was sure it was Hunter with Grace and Dane. So I bent down as I approached the two shadows on the sand, trying to hide in the tall grass.

"Oh, Hunter," a woman's voice moaned.

No, please, no. Immediately, I froze and peered between the tall grass.

He sat on the dune, his back to me. There was no mistaking the mustard shirt he had on. A woman sat on top of him, her skirt hitched up around her thighs as she straddled him, moving back and forth. I gasped, then quickly pulled my hand across my mouth. It was too late. She heard me and immediately stopped fucking him. Her stare locked on me. Then Hunter turned. Everything was happening in slow motion, and it chained me to the sandy bed.

"Lourde?"

My heart pounded, and anger flooded my veins. I dropped my heels. The thud pulled me out of my nightmare. Then I started to run.

"Fuck, get off me," I heard him say, followed by a shriek, then, "Lourde! Fuck! Wait." I was already putting the distance between us with every step I took. I pushed further, my thighs burning with each lunge forward.

"Wait, Lourde," he yelled, but I was faster and leaner than him. He wasn't catching up to me. Tears lapped my cheeks, and my hair flung across my face. Not again. This can't be happening again.

Déjà vu. *Why me?* Why do all the men I'm with cheat? Was it me?

I tripped on something in the sand, hurtling forward. Pain shot up my ankle, and I doubled over. *Shit!*

Hobbling back up, I didn't care how much it hurt. I had to keep going. Quickly testing my weight on it, I let out a gasp of pain but knew it wasn't broken. *Keep running, you fool. Just run.*

I don't know how long had passed, but I couldn't run anymore. My ankle throbbed, and my eyes clouded with tears. I'd run past the house and further away from Hunter and my friends.

Regaining my breath, I slid out my phone from my clutch. I tried Pepper, but her cell went to voicemail. *Dammit.* My last shot was Grace. It rang until it rang out—double shit.

All my stuff was back at the house. I could get it, but he might be there. Then what? I didn't have anywhere to go. Everything was booked out for the summer well in advance.

I wiped away the tears that stung my cheek. My brother would know what to do. I couldn't decide anything this frazzled. I clicked on Connor's name. After two rings, he picked up. "Lourde, what time is it?" He sounded half-asleep. Of course, he was. It was after midnight.

"I'm sorry, I need your help." I burst out crying again.

"What's wrong? Are you okay?" No longer sleepy, concern laced his voice.

"I'm okay. Hunter and a girl were at the beach, together... fucking!" The last word came out in an angry yell.

"That little weasel, I'll fucking kill him. Are you with the girls?"

"No, that's just it. I didn't want to go back to the party, so I just ran. I tried calling them, but they didn't pick up."

Silence rang down the line, then after a moment, he spoke, "Barrett."

"What?"

"Barrett's in the Hamptons. Text me your address and wait right there, okay?"

"Wha—"

The line went dead. I texted my location like he asked and waited.

Barrett's in the Hamptons. I sucked in a breath.

Almost immediately, my phone beeped.

Connor: *You can stay with Barrett. He will be there in five.*

Barrett? He was here? I was a miserable mess. I flashed back to my debutante, where he found me outside after finding a cheating Josh. Then the feeling of his brawny arms as he pulled me over the gearshift and onto his lap made me forget my ex. I thought he wanted to kiss me with the way fire burned behind his eyes. But I was so wrong. When he didn't make a move, I ran out, beyond humiliated.

Now he was coming to my aid again. How embarrassing. I swear I'm not a lousy fuck.

I wiped away the tears, ran my fingers through my hair, and stared down at the bright shade of tangerine on my manicured bare toes. *Shit!* Some lucky girl was about to score a pair of two-thousand-dollar heels come sunrise.

5

BARRETT

I just turned away my Hampton fuck who had arrived at the house to ride me till sunrise.

Connor rang, telling me Lourde had just witnessed her boyfriend fucking another woman, and after hearing that, I wasn't in the mood. I was fucking livid.

It was déjà vu.

Talk about getting dealt the shit end of the stick more than once. The poor girl had more heartache than Jennifer Aniston.

Quickly, I grabbed my keys, picking up the closest set on the keyholder, my black Audi R8. Good. I'd get to her sooner. The thought of Lourde alone on the streets had me testing the speed limits of the V10 engine and white-knuckling the steering wheel the entire way. Slowing down slightly to navigate the corner, I spotted a shadowy figure in a dark green dress on Windmill Lane. I slammed on the brakes and jolted forward. Killing the engine, I jumped out and walked toward her. "Lourde," I said in a low voice.

Shit. Lourde's arms were curled around the satin dress across her knees, and when she peered up at me, the whites of her eyes were tinged red. Mascara stained the tops of her cheeks, and tears pulled at the corners of her eyes. For a moment, I took her in. She wasn't perfectly made like the porcelain doll she always was. She was broken and so fucking perfect it hurt.

She wiped her nose with the back of her hand. "Barrett, can we just go, please?" As she pulled herself to a standing position, her dress opened, revealing a high slit to her mid-thigh. My dick hummed in my pants. What a fucktard Hunter the third, fourth, or fucking fifth was.

I opened the door for her, and she climbed in. *Where the fuck were her shoes?*

I didn't ask.

After closing her door, I slid inside and started the car up again, slamming the door shut. The engine roared as we went down the street.

"Thank you for coming, Barrett," she whispered.

"You don't need to thank me, Lourde. I'd do anything for you."

I felt her stare but kept my eyes pinned to the stretch of road. It was the truth.

"Connor's like family to me, which means you are too."

She sighed. "Yes, of course."

"What happened?"

With her voice almost at breaking, but she proceeded to tell me how her evening unfolded. How she saw Hunter and some slut in his lap on a dune, riding him and moaning like a cheap whore. Okay, maybe I added that last part.

By the time we got back to my home, my skin burned with rage. I pressed the remote, and the garage door rolled open. After I slid the car in, I killed the engine, stepped out, and opened her door. I slammed it shut, then turned to her. Her startled expression changed as she took me in.

"What is it, Barrett?" she asked as confusion splashed across her pretty face.

"I want to smash his face in, Lourde, for what he did to you."

Her eyes widened at my admission. "Get in line," she said, clutching her purse to her body.

Side by side, we rode the elevator in silence. Her attention was glued to the floor a million miles away. In the dim elevator lighting, my gaze fell upon her profile of a small nose, high cheekbones, and creamy skin. A dusting of freckles dotted her cheeks and the hollow of her neck. The last time we were this close was when I stupidly pulled her onto my lap all those years ago after her debutante ball. The night I wanted to kiss her bow-like lips but didn't dare.

I was about to say something when the doors pinged open. As I walked out of the elevator, I signaled her to follow. Arriving past the foyer and into the kitchen, I turned around. "What can I get you? Water? Coffee?"

She tossed her clutch on the counter, and I held my hand out, stopping it before it dropped to the ground. "Why me, Barrett? Why does this happen to me?"

Damn. She was asking me?

She made her way toward the kitchen counter. Under the lights, the satin clung to her waist, down her long legs, and between her thighs. *Fuck!* I should've taken that quick blow job earlier.

She sat on the bar stool. "Or are all men assholes?"

Strategically, I stood on the opposite side of the counter, needing that barrier between us.

Fuck, she was gorgeous. Even with her mascara-stained cheeks and glassy hazel eyes.

"All men are assholes. What can I say?"

"If you're trying to make me feel better, you're not helping." She put her head in her hands.

"Hey." I walked around and grabbed her hands. She glanced at me. Quickly, I dropped my hands and took a step back. *What the hell was that?*

"What I meant to say was, some of us cheat, some aren't built for love, and then there's the rest. They fit the mold and get married, mostly because society dictates they should."

She stood up and stepped toward me. Her hair smelled of salt and berries. Her eyes were black and smudgy like magnets drawing my gaze. "And which man are you, Barrett?"

"Easy, I'm the man not built for love. And the biggest asshole of all."

"Ugh." She turned away. "I need to sleep."

Truth hurts, sweetheart. Get used to it. "Follow me."

We walked in silence. The wood floor, soft against our bare feet, led to the large curved staircase in the center of the home. Of course, she was used to seeing beautiful homes. Probably grander and more stately than my home. I could've had just that, but I chose homey. I chose warmth over stark. Every little detail in the house I'd thought of— warm tones, paintings commissioned by not the best artists but painted pictures that spoke to me. Not that I'd ever admit to that. The boys would think I was a pussy. The furniture, picked for both comfort and style, dressed each room.

Down the large hallway filled with art and living plants, I led her to the guest suite. I turned the knob and opened the double French doors. "This is your room."

She stepped past me. Her bare arms grazed my chest. "This is nice, Barrett. Not what I expected at all."

What did she expect? I didn't want to get into a conversation with me standing outside her room and her dressed in barely anything.

"So, where's your room?"

"Down the other end." And the hell away from you.

"Well, do you have something I can wear?"

Oh, shit. "Let me see what I can find."

I started walking down the hallway, but when I turned, I found her behind me.

"I can bring it to you."

"I know." She smiled. Her grin sent a lifeline to my dick. *No. No. No.* Three ways saying the same thing meant the same answer. No touching Connor's sister. You're no good for her, and she's definitely not one to fuck and leave.

I heard her follow me inside, and without looking back, I quickly made my way to the walk-in closet. *Just grab anything, a t-shirt, sweats, anything to get her out of your bedroom.* I rifled through my oak drawers, trying to find something, anything.

Walking out with a bundle of t-shirts and shorts in my hands, I expected to find her in the doorway. Instead, she stood at the arched windows facing the ocean in the far corner. The moonlight shone, catching her wavy hair. From here, I could make the outline of her French undies and the bare curve of her ass.

What the hell, man. You need to get laid.

"This is magical."

"It's a nice view," I said, my tone clipped. "I've got some t-shirts for you."

"You built this place, right?"

"I restored it, stripped it back to its bare bones, keeping the best bits and making it whole again."

She turned to face me and took the clothes. Her hand brushed my thumb, and it sent a current down the base of my spine. I stood taller than her, a lot taller without her shoes too.

She stood on her toes and wrapped her arms around

38

my neck. "Thank you, Barrett," she said, kissing me on the cheek.

My arms wrapped around her lower waist, and her tits brushed against my chest, her smell intoxicating like candy apples. We stayed like this for too long. Letting my arms fall to the side, I said, "I think you should get some rest, Lourde. We'll figure the rest out tomorrow."

She turned on her heel without looking back. Grateful for her exit, I exhaled. Having her this close and all to myself was testing my strength.

6

LOURDE

All his shirts smelled woody with hints of vanilla, like Barrett. I slid the oversized t-shirt over my ass. Cloaked in his scent, I couldn't stop thinking about Barrett. It took my mind off Hunter.

As soon as my head hit the pillow, I texted the girls, letting them know where I was in case they sent out a search party. I also made it crystal clear to keep my location a secret from Hunter. The last thing I needed was for him to come back with some bull-shit excuse that no, it wasn't his dick in some wanna-be high society bimbo. After that, I turned my phone off. I needed to sleep off this nightmare.

Sliding into the high thread count sheets, I turned to my side, staring out the bay windows that framed the post-card view of the ocean. I remembered when Barrett bought the home in Montauk. Conner had mentioned it when they were both over for dinner a few years back. That kind of information Barrett wouldn't just offer. He was so private. He bought the worst house on the best street. That was what Connor had said. He couldn't understand why Barrett, with all this money, just didn't tear it down, preferring to renovate it and piece it back together, brick by brick. From my brief walk-through of Barrett's home, I could see why. The place was character-filled and homey, a feeling you couldn't just replicate if you tore it down.

I punched down another pillow again, trying to get comfortable. Like the last two times, I was having no luck with it. Okay, maybe it wasn't the goddamn pillow that was the problem.

Hunter the third. A cheater. Barrett Black. Not built for love. What the hell was wrong with the men of today? And why did I choose them?

Actually, I hadn't. My parents were setting me up with these men. I wasn't doing much of the choosing at all. Maybe that was the problem. They were so hell-bent on me marrying the right man from the right family so I could just get sucked back down the totem pole of the Diamond women. Be in my place. Act a certain way. *Blah Blah Blah.*

"Fuck!" I yelled into my pillow. Nothing about my life was making me happy. I was twenty-three, not thirty-three. This ought to be the best time of my life, but it was far from that. My name carried certain responsibilities, and the expectations of my parents, or rather my mom, were weighing me down.

A knock at the door pulled me upright. I dragged my fingers through my hair as the door opened.

"Lourde? Is everything okay?"

Barrett appeared in the doorway. His hair was tousled and unruly. *Had he not slept either?*

"Yes. Sorry, I just can't sleep."

"Did you say fuck?"

Geez, did this guy have the hearing of an owl?

"No, I just yawned… loudly," I added, so he didn't

think I was a loon.

"Okay, well, I'll let you—" he grasped the door handle.

"Actually, there is something."

He stepped in, his bare chest catching the moonlight. Curves of muscles ran down his long torso to his blue sweats that hung low, showing his delicious V. His body molded like a statue, rippled and cut. I rolled my lips together. Thank fuck it was dark. Sitting up, I urged him to sit on the edge of my bed. But he didn't move out of the doorway.

"I won't bite," I said, my frustration with men growing.

Slowly, he walked toward the bed, sitting on the edge. In the gray light, his features came into view. His five o'clock shadow dotted his square jaw and his smooth tanned skin looked like he'd spent the winter in the Bahamas instead of in Manhattan.

I leaned back, pulling my knees up. Barrett's shirt barely covered my thighs, but I didn't care. Maybe like Hunter's drunk friend said, perhaps I should color outside the lines. Heck, the flutter at the pit of my stomach when Barrett's gaze settled on my thighs was new and addictive.

"What is it, Lourde?"

His gaze crept higher up my thigh. *Did he find me attractive?* My skin warmed at the thought that maybe this wasn't as one-sided as I thought.

"Five years ago when I made my debut, do you remember that night?"

"Of course, you were with Josh."

I widened my eyes. "You remember his name?"

"Of course. I always remember a name." He blinked. "What about it?"

"You dropped me home that night."

"That's right." He held my gaze, and my breathing quickened. The air in the room changed. After all this time, I needed to know the truth, and suddenly this need to know overtook me. I was fed up with being the perfect daughter, the perfect sister, and the perfect girlfriend. It was now or never. I wanted to break perfection, starting now.

I sucked in a heady breath. "Did you want to kiss me?"

"Lourde." He raked his hand through his hair.

"I just want to know, Barrett."

He stood up quickly, moving to the foot of the bed. "I shouldn't be here. If your brother found out…"

"You don't strike me as the type to worry about what other people think."

"You don't know what kind of man I am." He stared down at me. His fiery stare trailed my body from my legs up to the curve of my breasts, where he hovered. *Fuck*. My body tensed. Fear laced my throat. My heart pounded. I didn't care what man he was. I wanted him to do filthy things to me. Filthy things that a girl like me shouldn't be interested in doing with my brother's best friend.

"What k… kind of man are you?" I stuttered out. My lungs emptied of air and made me feel dizzy.

"Sleep, Lourde."

He gave me one last stare before disappearing.

I slammed my head back into the pillow and pressed my hands to my cheeks.

What the hell was that? And why am I so turned on right now?

Barrett isn't dangerous. *Is he?* He'd always been quiet and mysterious, but never…

My lungs filled back up with the air, needing to quell my lightheadedness. I pulled the covers back over my bare legs. But I wasn't cold. My skin heated from head to toe, lit by his stare and his insatiable hooded eyes. There was no way in hell I'd sleep after that.

No fucking way.

I needed to know more.

7

BARRETT

Control. *Control it, Barrett.*

Waking up, I had the best hard-on known to man. With my dick between my hands and Lourde's creamy thighs on my mind, I came with a thundering release.

After answering all my emails, I went for a long run to clear my head. When I'd left, her door was closed. Presumably, she was still asleep. Connor's words played in my memory like a rerun as I pounded the sand. "Take care of my sister," he'd said on the phone.

Exactly, Barrett, listen to someone for once. Connor was the guy who got me into the position I was in today. He was the only guy willing to give a young upstart a go when he'd convinced his parents to work with a new property developer. *Their connections sold out your first development.* I owed him. Don't fuck up the relationship with Connor just because you want a taste of the forbidden fruit that lay between Lourde's legs.

I slapped my thigh, trying to breathe life back into my legs. They burned from sprinting miles along the sand. I pushed harder on the way back. Punishing myself was essential. Choosing the more strenuous workout and punishing myself had become a daily habit. Grueling and daily workouts were key to doing just that.

The sun dawned its new day. The ocean crashed against the shore, taking and sucking back the whitest sand with it. I focused on my meeting today and the site in East Hampton, a potential redevelopment that no one knew about but me with my connections. I didn't say they were all legitimate. But I wasn't afraid of a little dog fight, especially when money was involved. A whisper of an existing hotel going broke had me swooping in. Well, that was just good business. Too bad if others didn't see it that way. Today marked the beginning of finalizing that deal.

As much as my mind wanted to focus on the meetings today, they kept replaying the vision of her lying down on the bed. Legs pulled into her chest, my t-shirt skimming across her creamy thighs—she'd never looked so fuckable.

Those legs, I wanted to bite and kiss. Then when she'd moved and the hem of my t-shirt pulled up against her black-lace panties, I had to stand up and get the fuck out of there. She was a precious doll concealed in a devil's body. And I was Prometheus, wanting to steal her fire.

But I was no fucking good for anyone, most of all Lourde. She deserved better than a monster like me, a monster who didn't realize what was going on in his own family before it was too late.

I ran past the reeds and up the wooden pathway from the ocean to my home. The wind swirled, cooling the beads of sweat that clung to my chest.

Punching in the code, I pushed the gate open onto the front patio. Any other morning, I'd have dipped into the infinity pool and done some laps. Opening the slider, I shook off my sneakers, placed them on the shoe rack, and walked into the living room. Curved furniture pieces and my armchair upholstered from the comfiest fabric were where I spent a lot of my time. Most people just passed off designs on their interior decorators, and I won't lie, she did help me. But this house was my baby, and I hand-picked every piece of furniture, unlike my apartment in Manhattan. But that was more of a bachelor pad. This was a home where, if something was out of place, it didn't matter. I felt more relaxed here than in my home on the Upper West Side.

I walked past the floor-to-ceiling bookshelf separating the living room space from the kitchen.

A mouthwatering smell was coming from the kitchen. I don't remember booking my chef, but maybe my assistant, Aimee, did.

I rounded the corner. Lourde danced to the faint music. Her hips swayed, pulling the hem of my t-shirt daringly close to revealing the curves of her ass.

Fuck.

She hovered over the induction cooktop with her back to me, and I stopped, mesmerized by the beauty with wavy light brown hair moving like an angel of sin in my kitchen.

"Morning," I announced.

She spun around, and the motion whipped her t-shirt upward. My gaze fell to her thighs. Redness bloomed in her cheeks. "Barrett, you scared me!"

"I'm a scary guy," I said evenly.

She stalled, taking in my drenched shirt, then met me squarely in the eye.

"What's all this?" I looked past her to the sizzle on the hot plates.

"I raided your fridge. I, thought I'd make you breakfast."

She smiled before turning around, permitting me to stalk her ass.

Her toned legs beckoned me to run my hand up and down them. All I wanted to do was rip her black panties to the side and delve my fingers into her. I pushed my stool underneath the counter bar, hiding the thickness that formed in my Hugo Boss swim trunks.

She'd just be a fuck like the rest of them. Worse yet, she came with baggage. *Not. Worth. It.*

Sausages, poached eggs, and tomatoes with maple bacon colored the plates she placed in front of me.

"Are you trying to give me a heart attack?" I questioned her. Her shoulders rounded lower. "I'm kidding, Lourde. Thanks," I said, and a slight smile appeared on her lips.

Flecks of jade turned her eyes more green than hazel from the sunlight streaming in from the windows. Her small pointy nose and full bowed lips were naturally beautiful. It was here I took her in. Light freckles dotted the upper part of her porcelain cheeks. Her warm, golden, and naturally wavy hair, tumbled down to her mid-back.

"You're staring," she said.

"No, I'm not," I snapped back. "You have something on your face." I lied.

"Oh, do I?" She took her hand to her face and wiped off the imaginary fleck, embarrassed.

I may have chuckled. Yes, I was an asshole. "No, here." I reached for her hair and pretended to flick it away before she could see there was nothing in my hand. "All gone."

"Thanks." She held my gaze before I changed the topic.

"Well, I don't know about you, but I'm famished."

It only took me a few minutes to devour the entire contents of my plate, not having that many carbs and fried food in forever.

Looking up, I noticed her watching me. "Can I stay a little longer?" she asked.

My cutlery fell with a clank.

"It will just be for a few more days till I figure out what I'm going to do."

"Are you still thinking of staying out here for the summer?"

"Yes, my friends are here. I can't let Hunter stop me from having fun, but I'll just have to find somewhere to stay."

"You're kidding, right?" *Was she nuts?* The Hamptons were booked.

"Well, maybe Connor can pull some strings."

"How about the Diamond house?"

"It's still being renovated and sprawling with trades."

Dammit.

"Would it be that bad if I stayed here?" Her voice was soft, but there was a hidden dare in her eyes I couldn't ignore.

I needed to focus. Having Lourde here would be a distraction and a dangerous one at that.

"What would your brother say?"

"Let me deal with him. He'll be fine."

I glared at her.

"What brother is that?" I heard Connor's voice. Leaning back on my stool, he walked up the foyer with a shit-eating grin.

What the fuck?

"Connor?" she shrieked and hopped off the bar stool, giving her brother a huge hug.

Seeing them so close made me miss my sister. I hadn't seen her in months, blaming it on selling 21 Park, but the truth was, seeing her was so painful.

He dropped his duffle bag and threw his arm around her.

"What are you doing here?" she asked.

"What on earth are you wearing?" He took a step back, staring at her t-shirt, or rather mine that draped just below her butt, showing off her long legs.

"My clothes are in Hunter's room back at the house. And I couldn't go back there last night."

Connor strayed beyond his sister to me in the kitchen.

"Hey, man, I wasn't expecting you."

He walked over, casually dressed. I wondered why he wasn't running Diamond Incorporated with his overbearing father today.

He stared at the two plates. "She made breakfast." I shrugged.

"Jesus, why are you staring at him like that?" Lourde questioned. She saw his laser stare accusing me of something I hadn't done.

"You made breakfast, and you're in his t-shirt," he said.

"Jesus, Connor, calm down. As if I'd ever do anything with your baby sister," I said.

"Good, that's what I needed to hear."

Lourde narrowed her eyes but said nothing. "I didn't realize it was up to you, *brother.*"

He turned around. "When it's my best friend, it is," he snapped.

"Um, hello, don't you think I've had enough failed relationships to last a lifetime? And with Mr. Mysterious over there, puh-leeze."

Mr. Mysterious? A vein throbbed in my neck.

Connor laughed. "Barrett doesn't do relationships, Lourde."

"I love the unannounced visit, but why are you here and at eight in the morning?"

He picked up a slice of crispy bacon from Lourde's plate and ate it. "I thought my sister might need me."

"How about work? Did Dad flip about you leaving?" Lourde asked.

"No, I told him what happened with Hunter."

"Oh, great. And Mom now obviously knows. She'll be rubbing her hands together now, thinking of who she could pair me with next."

Lourde lowered her body onto the stool, her back curving as she slumped her shoulders.

I laughed. "Surely not."

"Mom, Dad, and I all want the best for you, Lourde. That's why they suggest certain men. There's no harm in that."

"There is when they all turn out to be cheating assholes."

"Mom mentioned she was having lunch with the Crawfords this week. Do you remember Harry from prep school?"

"You've got to be kidding me," she said.

I nearly spilled my macchiato. They were trying to set her up again. Talk about chained to the Diamond name.

"No, what?" Connor genuinely looked at her as though he didn't know why she was questioning him.

"Do I need to spell it out for you? It's been less than twenty-four hours since I saw Hunter's dick in another woman's sex hole."

I laughed, and Mr. Killjoy tossed me a scowl. "What? She has a point, Connor."

"Would you want the best for your sister, Barrett?"

"Of course."

Connor knew very little about my sister, Evelyn. Only what I'd told him which was that she lived in Boston. But that's all I gave him. No one knew our family secret, and my parents weren't alive to tell the tale. And Evelyn certainly didn't want to live through the trauma. She'd done that enough by retelling it to the best therapists I could find. Knowing my monster father abused her haunted me every day. Every damn day, I carried that guilt like the weight of a wall of bricks.

"As you can see, so do I."

"I appreciate that, brother, I do. But you can tell Mom that I won't be dating Harry or anyone else anytime soon. I'm single, it's summer, and you can't marry me off yet."

"I'll try."

Lourde sighed. "Okay, maybe tell her to give me the summer."

"I also came to tell you everything, and I mean, even the budget four-star hotels are completely booked out. So, unless you want to go crawling back to Hunter… which I suspect you don't, I suggest you come back to Manhattan with me."

"No! There's got to be something?"

"My secretary has called around, and I've put in some favors asking some guys I know. There's zero."

"She can stay here."

Dammit, Barrett.

"Really? Oh, thank you, Barrett." She swarmed toward me, her arms barely finding their way around my shoulders in an awkward hug.

"Fuck, Lourde, pull your arms down. I can see your ass."

Removing her arms, she giggled. "Sorry!"

She smelled of bacon and fried food as she hovered between my open legs on the bar stool.

Connor watched me. "I'll be out most of the time anyway, and the guest suite is at the other end of the house," I quickly added.

"That's generous, but I don't expect you to put her up."

"Hello! I'm right here. I can make my own decisions, and I say yes!"

I laughed. "Fuck, you try arguing with that," I added.

Connor shook his head. "Yeah, I'm at a loss."

"Great, so it's settled." A huge smile spread across her face. "Connor, can you stay today so we can celebrate the start of summer? Maybe have a few people around?" She looked up at me with doe-eyes. "You realize this house is perfect for parties, Barrett?"

"Hold up, Lourde. I said you could stay, not have a bunch of strangers around, invading my space."

"Barrett is very private, Lourde, but maybe a few people would be okay?" Connor raised his eyebrows. "We could call it a celebration for selling your award-winning tower."

"Oh, sorry, Barrett, with everything going on, I forgot to congratulate you on selling 21 Park."

"How did you know?" Connor and I said at the same time.

"It's just the most prestigious tower in all of Manhattan. How could I not know? Plus, it popped up on my news feed."

Surprised she had an interest in architecture, I caved.

"Okay, maybe a few people." I flicked my wrist. "Shit. I have to run, make yourselves at home. And I'll ask the housekeeper to set up your room, Connor."

"Thanks, bud. I'll head back tomorrow. Tonight I'll let off some steam and have fun with my sister and my best friend. And maybe a few lady friends."

I smiled. "Sounds good." I turned around, acutely aware the only lady friend I wanted to fuck was his sister. But Lourde wasn't fucking material, and my meat stick couldn't go anywhere near her.

8

LOURDE

"Tell me you're not going back to him?" Grace asked.

"Of course not," I said.

"You'd be crazy to after his dick was inside another woman. Right?" Pepper questioned, slightly wobbly on her six-inch heels.

We were on our third champagne, standing around the kitchen counter with music blaring, bodies dancing, and laughter sounding against the backdrop of the ocean.

Okay, so the little party I planned at Barrett's went slightly viral, and by viral, I mean, friends and friends of friends had driven from Manhattan to Barrett's oceanfront mansion.

Connor and Barrett were on the balcony, gorgeous women hovering around them. In particular, my gaze kept finding Barrett and the brunette that hung off him like a leech.

Taking my champagne to my lips, I stared at him from across the room—his height, easy to pick out amongst a room full of people. Black shirt with sleeves rolled up, his thick black-brown hair neatly brushed the tops of his ears, and I imagined running my hands through it. He glanced over his shoulder as though sensing my heated thought. Quickly, I glanced away, embarrassed he found me pining over him.

"Hello, Lourde?" The champagne slid down my throat, and I diverted my attention toward Pepper, who was looking at me expectantly.

"What?" She followed my previous line of sight. "If I never see Hunter again, I'll be the happiest woman alive," I added, and it was the truth.

Pepper looked at Grace. "So, you're staying here, then?"

"Well, there's nowhere else."

"And Barrett is okay with that?" Grace questioned.

"Don't you mean, is Connor okay with you shacking up with his best friend?" Pepper elbowed me in the ribs, her gaze drifting to Barrett, where she'd caught me staring a moment ago.

"Connor's fine with it. Barrett's eight years older than me. What would he want with me anyway? You've seen the women he's with. Just look over there." I tilted my head toward the balcony, where he rested against the wall.

"You sound jealous." Pepper tossed her jet-black hair over her shoulder.

I huffed out a groan. "Anyway, he's here for work, not a vacation. I'll hardly see him."

"Hmm," Grace added.

"Ugh, just say it, you two."

"You crushed on him hard. I just don't think that's changed," Pepper said.

"Well, he *is* gorgeous. It's just a silly little crush played out in my head because I knew it could never come true."

"Maybe it can," Grace lowered her voice.

The possibility sent a tingle up my spine. "Well, he came to my room last night."

"What the hell?" Pepper blurted out.

"Nothing happened. I think he was just checking on me. I made this sound in my pillow, and he stuck his head in to see if I was alive, I think."

"Checking on you… what guy does that, ever?" Pepper questioned.

"Anyway, what happened?" Grace asked, ignoring Pepper.

"Nothing happened." I smacked my lips together, remembering his gaze as it drifted up my thighs.

"But…" Grace pushed.

"But, if I'm honest, he scared me and thrilled me at the same time."

"There's this darkness to him," Pepper added.

"He isn't like the other guys in the group." We turned and gazed at the four of them, who were now hovering in the living room.

"Look at the four of them. Arrogant, gorgeous assholes. I think they're hunkholes," Pepper said.

"Hunkholes?" I popped an eyebrow at the term.

"Hunky assholes," Pepper said.

We all fell into raucous laughter. "I love that," Grace added.

"Ew, don't call my brother a hunk!" I screwed my face up.

"Hate to break it to you, but he's cute, always has been, and by the lineup of women around the four of them, I'm not the only one noticing." Pepper shrugged.

"They're like a swarm of bees." My eyes narrowed on the four women who surrounded them.

"There you are." Jake patted Pepper on the ass, and Dane wrapped his arms around Grace.

"Hey, Lourde, sorry about you and Hunter. You know Hunter can be a jerk," Dane said.

"Thanks, Dane." The image of him on the dunes with another woman riding him came rushing back in.

"You know, for what it's worth, he's completely distraught about what happened."

Distraught? "I'm sure he is," I said, keeping my voice level.

"Where is he anyway?" Pepper asked.

"He knew he couldn't come here," Jake added.

"Hell, no," I spat out, the pitch of my voice higher than usual.

"He's at another party."

Phew.

"Have you returned his calls? He said he's been trying to call you all day," Pepper asked.

"No. Why would I?"

"He's miserable. Maybe just hear the guy out."

"Not a chance."

"I have to agree with Grace," Pepper said, and her comment surprised me. "The guy's a class A dickwad, but you should still speak to him, at least tell him to fuck off and end the relationship once and for all.

"I'll think about it." Turning to Dane and Jake, I said, "Anyway. I hope we can all still be friends."

"Of course, Lourde." Dane nudged me, his strength nearly tipping me over while Jake smiled.

* * *

Needing some fresh air and some time away from overly affectionate couples, I walked outside past the pool toward the handrail, soaking in the warm breeze and soothing ocean.

"Pretty girls shouldn't be out here on their own."

Barrett's low voice pulled me out of my haze. He handed me a champagne flute and slid beside me, staring out at the sea.

"Is that so? Sorry, I didn't expect this many people here. I only invited a few, and word got around."

"I don't think it was all you're doing." He turned, his gaze settling on Connor, who was in his element with his group of friends in the corner of the living room.

"Why aren't you with them?" I asked, noticing his toned golden forearms resting on the metal handrail.

"Socialites aren't my thing."

I raised my eyebrow. *He was kidding, right?* He, Connor, Ari, and Magnus—before he got married—had women hanging off their arms every weekend.

"Socialites with an agenda," he clarified.

"Ah." Made sense.

"And those girls have an agenda. I'm straight up with women. I get what I need, and so do they."

I rolled my eyes. "So romantic, Barrett."

"Fuck romance, Lourde. Look where that got you." His stern voice leveled me. His gaze pierced a hole in my exterior.

"Guess you're used to gentlemen."

"Of course." I swallowed down the thickness lining my throat. "But look how far that got me."

"Maybe I ought to be more like you. Romance and me go like kryptonite to Superman."

He laughed, shaking his head. His hair tossed with the stiff breeze that rode to shore.

Maybe you could be the distraction I need.

"You're romance overload, Lourde. I bet you have Mr. Darcy tucked underneath your pillow."

"Are you daring me to be bad, Mr. Black?"

"You don't know what bad is." His voice was low and steady, calling to my insides.

"Maybe you can show me," I whispered straight back.

He tilted his head down, and his lips were close to mine. Dark eyes held mine in a trance, completely oblivious to the party going on around us. After a beat, he opened his mouth to speak. "Not a chance," he said, then walked away.

Asshole.

* * *

It was well after midnight. Maybe I was sulking in the corner. Maybe I was slightly drunk. What was the goddamn difference?

Pepper and Grace left with their boyfriends, saying their goodbyes not before we organized a shopping trip tomorrow. I neglected to tell them about my earlier chat with Mr. Fucking Hot and Mysterious, which melted a hole in my underwear. That one I'd keep close to my chest. Once in a while, maybe tell myself that exchange happened.

The sizable crowd had dispersed, leaving Connor, Barrett, a few guys, and a handful of women around them.

I pushed away my champagne. I'd had enough rejection in the last twenty-four hours to last a lifetime, and Barrett's dismissal was just smearing salt on the wound. Since our earlier exchange, he'd completely forgotten the way he looked at me and was hitched with the leggy brunette who hadn't left his side. She was draped on his arm, hanging off him like a leaf on a thick branch. Her hand not so subtly rested on his thigh while he threw back his beer.

I watched him laugh and joke with Connor—both

carefree, living the lives they want and not caring about others around them. Their show was wearing thin. Walking out onto the balcony, I knew the fresh air would straighten me out. One breath of fresh air, then bed. Tomorrow I'd start my true vacation. Sun, surf, sand, and shopping. Everything the Hamptons was and more.

I checked my phone. Three missed calls from Hunter flashed on my screen.

Ugh. I'd eventually have to call him back, but tonight, I wanted to melt into my haze and just forget about it all. I wrapped my arms around my body. My halter dress with the exposed back, not doing anything to keep me warm from the now crisp air.

"Need a jacket?"

Turning around, a guy around my age took off his blazer and wrapped it around my arms.

"Thank you," I said, shouldering into the stranger's jacket. Perhaps this was the man to forget everything. Take a page out of the hunkholes book. No romance, just fucking. I laughed. How ridiculous. *I wasn't like that, was I?*

"Something funny?"

Did I laugh out loud? Damn, girl, you're drunk.

"Yeah, I'm not that girl."

"What girl?"

"Those girls," I said, turning around. My gaze settled on Barrett and the surrounding girls.

His eyes collided with mine. Anger burned behind them. *What was his problem?*

"Well, they *are* pretty but not my type."

My focus settled on the man in front of me. Blue eyes stared back. He was cute, definitely cute.

"Plus, I think you're way more beautiful than those girls. I'm Tom."

"Lourde." I smiled. Maybe I could go through with this after all.

I didn't know how long had passed when Connor appeared behind the cute guy. making me feel all fuzzy.

"Sis."

"Heyyy, Connorrr," I slurred. *Did I have that much cham-pagne?* How hadn't I noticed the other drink in front of me? Had he put that on the ledge of the balcony when he'd given me his jacket?

The fresh air was definitely not working to straighten me out as I'd hoped.

"And look, Barrett's here too, and your bew… ti… ful women."

"I don't think she needs another drink." Connor looked at what-was-his-name? Tim, Tom? I'd already forgotten.

"No, of course not. I didn't realize she was your sister, Connor."

"Sure you didn't," Barrett piped up.

"Go away, hunkholes!" I groaned.

"Hunkholes?" Barrett's brunette laughed. "Is that what you just said?"

"Yeah, what's it to you, social climber?"

"Lourde! Okay, someone needs to go to bed and sleep it off. Barrett, can you help Lourde to her room?"

Slutty girl, also known as Barrett's date, glared at me, and I glared back.

"Jess, help me clear out everyone. Party's over." He turned to the leggy brunette in the skimpy dress next to him. "Sure, then what?" she asked, hopeful.

"You and your friend, Scarlett, can hang back with Barrett and me. Cool, Barrett?"

"Sure," Barrett said, helping me out of the jacket.

What, so they could get laid, but I couldn't?

"I'd like my friend to stay, too," I said, fluttering my eyes at him seductively.

Barret balled the guy's jacket and thrust it back into his chest.

"No!" Barrett and Connor said at the same time.

"Oh, another time then. I guess I'll call you, Lourde," he said.

"Sure," my brother said sarcastically, then turned to Barrett.

"Let's go, Lourde."

Why were they cock-blocking me? *I was totally fine!*

My shoe hit the substantial sliding door threshold, propelling me forward. A hand snaked around my waist, jerking me back. Okay, maybe I wasn't totally fine, and why was Barrett's hand still resting on my hip after we got to the top of the staircase?

"You can go back to your date. You know I'm perfectly fine."

"There's nothing fine about you, Lourde."

"You know, there was nothing wrong with that guy down there."

"Did you know his name?" He walked beside me, his warm fingers digging into my skin.

"What?"

He spun me around. His dark eyes burned holes into me. I stepped back, and he took a step closer. I took another step back, hitting the bedroom door. He towered over me.

"You heard me." He was so close. His breath was on my face. I glared up at him. My heart thundered and clapped at his proximity.

"I can't remember his name," I said in a horse whisper.

His eyes trailed down to my lips, and I tilted my chin up slightly. *Kiss me.*

"Don't fuck around, Lourde. It's not you."

I straightened, brushing my chest against his. He stilled. "Go back to your date, Barrett. She's waiting."

With my hand behind me, I felt for the doorknob and opened it. He stood there watching as I shut it behind me.

Ugh! He wanted me. He didn't want me. His words didn't match his actions. If he wanted to play that way, I could too. I could be the temptation he can't ignore.

Maybe this summer started off on the wrong foot, but it sure as hell wouldn't go to waste.

9

BARRETT

"So much for having a few people round!" Connor slapped me on the back, spilling my macchiato across the marble counter.

"What the fuck, Connor?" Smoothing down my white shirt, I searched for any evidence of the spill. Lucky for him, it was clean.

"Shit, sorry!" he said, attempting to wipe up the spill but smearing it further around.

"Christ, give it here." I grabbed the sponge from his hands and meticulously wiped it clean. Has he ever cleaned anything in his life? He was so undomesticated. It was pathetic.

"What a party, huh? Who knew girls could pull together a party in a few hours?"

After washing my hands, I sat back down on the stool. "You're kidding, right? The Diamond women are experts at throwing parties."

"Yeah, I guess. I didn't realize Lourde had the gift. She managed music, catering, décor, and all in the space of six hours. Pretty impressive."

"Did you have fun with Jess?" I shot up an eyebrow. Since I'd known Connor, we'd always tried to one-up each other on the women we bed. "And where is she?"

"She's long gone. I sent her packing after we fucked for the third time." He grinned. "She gave me her number. Apparently, she's a doctor here. Who knew?"

"Are you going to call her?"

He squared his shoulders. "No," he said.

I laughed. "Good for you, bud."

I sipped on the rest of my remaining coffee. Fuck, it was cold. I needed to wake the fuck up and make another.

"How was…" Connor sat down, flicking through his phone.

"Scarlett," I said, never forgetting a name. I pressed the button on my overpriced coffee machine. The machine purred quietly.

I turned around and grinned. "Scarlett was fucking amazing." He didn't need to know that when I closed the door, she stripped down to barely anything before she passed out, cold. She slept it off on my daybed by the window, then I sent her home with my driver before everyone woke up. He didn't need to know I imagined it was Lourde stripping down to nothing in front of me. Fuck, no, he certainly didn't need to know that.

"Oh," he grinned, "Don't we have it all?"

"That we do."

Lourde rounded the corner. Dressed in satin shorts and a camisole that showed the outline of her tits, I dragged my eyes quickly to the scowl that was set across her porcelain face. She walked toward me, grabbing a cup. She put it beside mine under the coffee machine. "Well, so glad to hear you guys got your rocks off last night. Lucky for some, huh?"

I straightened. "Morning," I said, keeping it light.

Since our exchange last night at the party where she tempted me, the minx couldn't escape my mind, and I thought about every way I could take her in this house—on the sofa, on the cool marble counter, in my oversized shower, and even in the goddamn tub.

What the fuck is wrong with me?

I grabbed my coffee from the machine and moved away from her. I had to leave before I thought about her anymore.

"Well, we weren't drunk and out of our heads," Connor said, not looking up from his screen.

"I wasn't drunk." She thrust a hand on her hip.

I widened my eyes, and she scowled at me. "Anyway, maybe I needed to let off a bit of steam, you know, with what happened and all."

Was she glaring at me?

"Not with a stranger, sis," Connor said, eventually looking up from his phone.

"He wasn't a stranger."

"What was his name?" I asked, lifting the lid off the glass jar filled with keto bites and popping one into my mouth.

Her scowl formed the slightest wrinkle on the bridge of her nose.

"It was Jax," she said, folding her arms.

I laughed. "Sure it was." She couldn't lie if her life depended on it. "I think you mean Tom."

"Whatever," she huffed out, running her hands through her hair.

"I'm sure you don't remember every single woman you bed."

"Me? No," Connor said, shaking his head. "But Barrett does… every single one. It's truly a gift."

"He's right. I never forget a name." Ever since I could

remember, I've made an effort to know and recall names. A simple thing like that got you noticed, especially when trying to climb the ranks as a youngster amongst the wealthy.

She groaned and turned around. A shade of crimson bloomed at the nape of her neck. I smirked. There was something about getting under her skin that got me off.

"Fucking around isn't a good idea, sis. We're men." Connor put his phone down, glaring in her direction.

I pushed my chair out. "Hell, I'm leaving that one alone."

"Don't start me with the sexist rhetoric, Connor. I'm reaching my threshold with it. Especially from you *and* Mom."

"It's for your own good. You know we all love you. Don't go trying to change the status quo that's existed in this family for generations."

I kept out of their family business, but I could sense her chomping at the bit to scream from the rooftops. Shit, I would. I'd never say that to my sister. She'd endured enough for any lifetime.

"Anyway, let's not argue. I'm heading back. Last chance to come back with me?" Conner asked.

She glanced at me. "I'll stay here for now. Something will come up soon. Don't worry. I won't cock-block you, Barrett."

I laughed. "Oh, I know that." I held her gaze too long before looking away. "You can stay as long as you like."

I turned to Connor. "See ya, bud. Let's catch up when I'm back in Manhattan. My nine o'clock is waiting."

"Count me in. Hey, wait up a second, I'll walk you out."

Walk me out? *Fuck.*

Grabbing my phone and keys off the counter, I headed for the door.

"Sis, make me another?" he said over his shoulder.

Standing out front, I turned to him. "Now I know you don't want to kiss me goodbye, honey, so what is it?"

He lifted his head, obviously deep in thought. "It's Lourde. This behavior has to stop right here, right now. She can't be bringing stray men back here, Barrett."

"So, what do you want me to do about it? I'm not a fucking bodyguard."

"I know, and you've done enough by letting her stay here. But man to man, keep an eye on her, please."

Concern etched on his face, but I didn't care. I had a job to do, and it wasn't being her babysitter.

"I'm at work all day."

"It's the nights I worry about, especially now that she's the single one and her friends are all shacked up."

"She's twenty-three, Connor."

"And still a Diamond daughter and sister. She can have fun but just not the type of fun you and I have."

Ah, and there it was. The precious reputation is what he cared about, making dirty Diamond headlines and fucking up everything.

"I'm no babysitter," I echoed.

"Just please, you're all I have out here," he said, desperation lacing his voice.

I checked my Cartier watch. "Jesus, fuck. Okay, I'll watch her. Now I really have to go."

"Thanks," he said, and I walked toward the car.

"Oh and, Barrett?"

"What the fuck is it now?" I turned around, and his eyes darkened.

"Don't fall in love with her."

I laughed. "You're kidding, right? Fuck me."

Opening the door, I slid into my midnight blue Aston Martin Vanquish, realizing my heart was beating ridiculously fast.

10

LOURDE

White paneled walls, chic blues, and timber floors fit out the rows of glass-fronted shops. Lilacs and creamy white hydrangeas colored the sidewalks, filling the streets with their faint sweet perfume.

All morning we'd roamed the village-like shops in East Hampton, buying anything that took our fancy, and in the process, we'd worked up a ravenous appetite. I'd bought three summer dresses, cut-off short shorts, and hit up Polo Ralph Lauren for some essentials. "Gosh, I'm in love with these," I said, holding up my new purchase of white denim shorts.

"I don't think I've ever seen you buy anything remotely that scandalous before." Grace smirked. Folding them back into my bag, I sipped on my frothy Frappuccino, unable to hide my smirk.

Pepper side-eyed me. "Why the slutty purchase?" she asked, picking at her wasabi chicken salad.

"I'm free, girls." I popped a piece of seared tuna in my mouth.

"On that, have you called him back?" she questioned.

"Who?"

Her brows shot up into her forehead. "Your ex, who else?"

Grace giggled, and Pepper's catlike eyes narrowed.

Since prep, these girls have had my back, and I loved them to the ends of the earth, but I wasn't calling him back. I didn't care what Pepper had to say about it.

"As if," Grace said. "Don't you dare."

"Yeah, what she said." I nodded.

"You know, he is pretty upset. He's moping about the house, complaining to Grace and me. He wants to see you."

I put my fork down and folded my arms. "And what did you say?"

"Once you visit another honey pot, the queen leaves," Grace interjected. "That's what I said, Lourde." I shot her a wink as she sipped on her French Earl Grey.

Pepper rolled her eyes. "I was more tactful."

"Tactful? Whose side are you on?"

"Don't look at me like that. Of course, I think what Hunter did was completely wrong. I just think you should talk to him, that's all. You were together for over a year."

"And that went up in flames in a matter of moans and orgasms. Although I doubt Hunter made her come." I took a deep breath. I think I was angrier that it happened to me again rather than losing Hunter.

"Do we know who she was?" I asked quietly.

"Her name is Bessy Miles. Lives in Manhattan, she's an influencer," Pepper said.

"In what?"

"Don't know. Let's see." Pepper slid her phone out as Grace flipped hers over. It was a race to find her on socials.

"I'll check TikTok," Pepper said.

"I've got Insta," Grace added.

I stirred and drank the remaining foam on the bottom of my Frappuccino.

Maybe I owed him a callback. *But what would I say?* It's over. Never call me again? He'd likely try to wrangle his way out of it like he always did when we argued—manipulating me and turning it around, so he seemed more the victim than the instigator.

But why would he want me back? Deep down, I knew we weren't compatible. If he wanted to get back with me, I seriously doubted it was because he loved me. Since I was old enough to have a boyfriend, indirectly or directly, I'd been set up with the wrong man. A man from a respectable family who somehow could benefit the Diamond empire.

Mom thought it was best for everyone because it worked out so well for her and her mother before her. Having both arranged marriages, the net worth and status of each family involved soared from the arranged unions.

But that wasn't me, was it? Married when she was just twenty-one, Mom never worked. She was the glue that held this family together, and Connor and I were so close because of her. I sighed. Lately, I felt like more of an outsider from the family than I ever had, all because I considered working and disagreed with being married off.

"Three and a half million followers on TikTok," Pepper said.

"For what?"

"She's a dancer."

"Don't you mean stripper? Britney Spears wears more clothes than her. Check out her Insta." Grace thrust her phone in front of me, and of course, I took it.

What did she have that I didn't?

I flicked the three-by-three square tiles that told her story. She was pretty if you were into Brazilian bottoms and tiny waists. Exotic, with tight black curls and honey skin. "She's pretty."

"Anyone's pretty with the right lighting." Pepper put her phone down, placing her hand on my arm. "Just think about returning his call. I think you might give him hope with the silent treatment, and if that's not your intention, then just call it off."

"Oh, it's off all right," I said, pushing away Grace's phone.

"It just sucks we're not in the same house anymore." Grace flicked her copper curl over her shoulder.

"Yeah, I guess," I said, not feeling as letdown about it as they were.

Pepper and Grace exchanged glances. "But it must be okay living on billionaire's row?" Pepper asked.

"It's a gorgeous house. I'm not complaining," I said, keeping it casual.

"Hmm, and how's the company?" Grace questioned.

I paused, unsure of how I actually felt about Barrett's company. Over the last two days, I wasn't sure if he wanted to kiss me or kill me. "Fine," I added.

Grace held her hand in the air, signaling the waiter for the check.

"Fine!" Grace laughed. "McHotty was checking you out a few times."

A flush of heat swept up my neck. *I didn't imagine it.*

"Well, he's a playboy. That means nothing," I said, even though I felt it meant something.

"Yes, it was hard to miss the women around them last night," Grace added.

"Connor and Barrett each had their fuck buddies for the night," I said. A jerky hand movement by Pepper had both Grace and I staring at her.

"What? It was a bug." She glared back. I always

thought Pepper was overly interested in Connor, but since she seemed blissfully happy with Jake, I thought she had forgotten about him.

Overhearing Barrett and my brother talking about their pleasurable nights was irritating. Not only because they cock-blocked me from having the same nondescript, no-strings-attached pleasure—which I'd never had—but also because even though I knew Barrett fucked around, bearing witness to it stung. Maybe, if I'm honest, a little more than catching Hunter cheat, which sounded so utterly ridiculous.

"Fucking hunkholes," Grace added, and we doubled over in laughter.

"You know, I think I might have called them that to their face when I was drunk."

"Fuck. No." Pepper giggled.

I nodded.

"Ladies." The waitress placed the leather binder with the check in front of Grace.

She pulled out her black American Express and handed it to him to tap. "So I better run. Dane is waiting for his fellatio of dessert," she said, smiling. The waiter eyed her as he handed her card back before walking away.

Pepper and I laughed. "Should we meet up later?" She slid her card back into her Louis Vuitton purse and stood, gathering her bags.

"What did you have in mind?" I asked.

"Dinner at the Inn, then a party in Montauk. Dane's sister has a friend hosting on Lane Street."

"I'm in for dinner, but I might sit the party out."

"Oh, why? You're single. You should definitely mingle," Pepper exclaimed.

"Yeah, at least before your mom pairs you off with someone else," Grace added.

"Maybe for a drink then." The girls were right. I didn't want to get hitched up again. I needed to let my hair down. Maybe even meet someone and take him back to Barrett's. That would really drive him mad. *Ha.*

"What are you smiling about?" Pepper asked, getting up.

"Nothing." I scooped my bags onto my wrist and stood.

"You're such a dirty liar."

"I don't know what you're talking about." I giggled as I followed them out of the restaurant. God, if they only knew what dirty things I wanted to do.

* * *

So one drink turned into three at the party, and on the short ride back to Barrett's, I was feeling slightly buzzed. I blotted on some lip gloss as I exited the Uber and approached the house.

I hadn't seen Barrett since this morning. It wasn't like I expected him to be waiting for me or anything. I smoothed down my new summer dress. Cinched at the waist, it hugged just below my mid-thigh and was shorter than most of my other dresses. Pairing it with needle-thin stilettos, I fucking loved it.

I walked into the foyer and noticed a light coming from the living room. *Was he up?*

It was after eleven, but if Barrett was up, it couldn't hurt looking my best. He was only used to models and gorgeous women. I wouldn't put myself in that class. I ate, for starters. Be it a tuna salad paired with a Frappuccino, I may skimp on one thing, but I didn't go without. I also took care of myself, working out most days in the gym at home or taking spin classes.

My heels clicked against the wood floor. He wasn't in

the kitchen. I dropped my key on the counter, where the stools were tucked neatly underneath.

"Lourde." My heart thundered as he rounded out my name. My gaze fell to the living room. Barrett sat in the armchair with his laptop in the dimly lit corner. Behind him, the ocean crashed as the moonlight lit up a line of the ocean floor.

"You scared me, Barrett." It wasn't dark in here, but it certainly wasn't lit up either. The lighting felt more intimate now he was here. I walked toward him, swaying my hips ever so subtly. He wore gray sweats and a fitted black t-shirt. His tanned forearms were exposed and rested on the arms of the chair.

Slowly, his gaze drifted from my face to my breasts, down to my waist, landing on my thighs. My body thundered. One look and he'd doused me in kerosene, ready for lighting.

"You shouldn't be wearing that," he said through a pinched expression.

"What? You're not serious?" That was the last thing I expected after that fiery gaze. I kicked off my heels and threw my bag on the couch. I was fucking livid.

"*Deadly* serious."

"You're an asshole, you know." Breathless, I shoved my hand on my hip.

"I know." He kept staring at me.

"And what's wrong with this?" Purposely I twirled, slowly turning around with my hands outstretched before standing in front of him with my legs crossed.

He lowered his laptop screen.

"You don't normally wear things like that." He raked his teeth on his bottom lip.

"Well, all men like to see a bit of skin. Don't they?" I was skirting a dangerous line, one I wasn't sure I could follow through on. "Case in point. You and those women last night."

"I don't want all men to see your skin."

"So you and my brother can have all the fun, but I can't?"

He smiled. Like he'd won at some game. My skin hummed, and my veins flushed with rage.

Asshole. But I wasn't one to back down without a fight.

"Perhaps I ought to show some more skin." With my hands in a claw grip, I pulled at my hem, shifting it higher up on my thighs.

Before I knew it, he was standing in front of me, both hands squeezing my wrists still.

"Don't," he said, his pupils dilated, so the ring of green in his eyes was mostly black. His strength sent shivers up my arm.

"What are you going to do about it?" I said in a husky voice I didn't know I had, wondering if we were still talking about my choice of clothing or something else.

He stood, still squeezing my hands firmly in place, and glared down at me. His hooded eyes dropped to my lips, then back up to my eyes. I wanted to run my hand across his angular jaw and sharp nose and plant my lips on his in a dirty all tongue kiss.

"Nothing," he said, letting go of my hands and sitting back down. He flipped his laptop back open.

"Exactly," I said, completely and overwhelmingly left raw and untouched.

I'd never craved a man more in my entire life. I needed his hands on my skin the way they blazed and set my skin alight. Barrett had to be my fun. My escape. If he didn't want anyone else to touch me, then he had to do it. He could be my fuck buddy for the summer. Too bad my stupid crush was one-sided. *Wasn't it?*

I marched up the circular staircase, making sure my footsteps were elephant loud, and headed straight for the shower, scrubbing his touch off me in an effort to stop thinking about him.

Frustrated, pent up, and left wanting more, I curled up into bed. Then everything faded to black.

* * *

His lips trailed my neck, eventually landing on my mouth. Softly at first, then with an overwhelming desire, our tongues collided. I heard him moan my name. Lourde.

"Lourde."

There it was again. *Was I still dreaming?*

"Lourde?" A crushing weight landed on my body. I tried moving, but I couldn't. My dream drifted away, replaced by overwhelming fear. Suddenly, I opened my eyes, blinking and adjusting to the darkness. A familiar face was on top of me. I wasn't dreaming.

Hunter?

I screamed, but he quickly stifled it with both hands across my mouth.

"Lourde, shh, please. It's just me."

What the fuck? How did Hunter get in? He pressed me down, sandwiching me with his legs and weight as I tried unsuccessfully, squirming out from underneath him.

"Stop it. I'm not here to hurt you. You just haven't returned my phone calls."

His hand was still over my mouth, and my heart beat rapidly.

"I just want to say I'm sorry. I really am, and I can't be without you."

He stared into my eyes. I didn't care if he was sorry or

not. Scaring the life out of me in the middle of the night wasn't the way to do it.

"Okay, I'm going to take my hand off now. I want to kiss you. Please, hun."

No! Nausea swirled in my stomach as a scream formed in the back of my throat. Maybe now was my chance. I stopped wriggling, so he knew he could trust me. Slowly, he lifted his hands off my mouth, but before I could scream, he kissed me. His lips were wet. He tasted of whiskey. Shit, he was drunk, and now I was terrified. I turned to the side, but he shoved my face back into his. "No, please!" I yelled.

I closed my eyes, hoping this was an awful nightmare when suddenly he got the memo, and his crushing weight was off me. A loud whack followed, and I opened my eyes.

"What the fuck!" I heard Hunter groan as I shuffled up.

Barrett had him by the collar and punched him in the nose.

"Fuck!" he cussed.

I leaped out of bed. "How dare you, Hunter," I screamed.

He grabbed his nose, trying to stop the bleeding with his hand.

Barrett stood between him and me. "Are you all right, Lourde? Did he hurt you?"

"I'm fine," I said. "Just terrified is all."

"I love you, baby," he said, trying to get up.

With one fell swoop, Barret kicked him, and he fell back. "Get the fuck back down," he said, his voice razor-sharp.

"Jesus, man, I just want to speak to my girl."

"Your girl? I'll never be your girl," I yelled. "It's so over, Hunter. I never want to see you again!"

"Lourde, do you want to press charges on this little

cocksucker?" Barrett asked, pulling him up by the scruff of his shirt.

"Oh no, hun, please no. My family would disown me." He rubbed his forehead. "My father, fuck." Barrett's towering height dwarfed him.

God, he looked so pathetic. I really saw him for the asshole he was. Never in the year we'd been together had I truly craved his touch or loved his company. He was pleasant enough, but that was all.

"It's your call, Lourde, but nothing would give me more pleasure than to lock this creep up."

I walked toward him. Barrett extended his arm, his hand landing on my thigh. "Don't come any closer, Lourde," he said, pushing on my thigh.

Ignoring the warmth of his hand, I brushed past him, purposefully disobeying him and standing toe-to-toe with Hunter.

"No charges, but I'm not doing this for you, asshole. I'm doing it for *my* family."

"You heard the lady. Get the fuck out before I call the cops for breaking and entering."

Blood dripped down the front of his shirt, and he pinched the tip of his nose shut.

"I'm going."

"No shit, dickhead." Barrett pushed in front of me. My gaze was set on the curves of his shoulder and the lines of his ribs, realizing he was shirtless.

"You break into my house again, and you'll be wishing for the cops after I'm done with you."

Hunter scoffed and stalked his way out the doors with Barrett close behind him.

Pacing the bedroom, I replayed what had just happened. I felt sick to my stomach when I heard Barrett re-enter.

"He's gone, and he definitely won't be coming back. I sent him a parting message."

I lowered my head and wrapped my arms around the cool of my satin camisole. *What if Barrett hadn't pulled him off me in time?*

"Fuck, you're shivering, Lourde."

Before I could look back up, he was next to me, helping me down on the bed and wrapping a blanket around my shoulders.

"I thought I was dreaming." I glanced at Barrett. A blush crept up my neck, then I blinked it away, hoping he didn't notice. "I woke up and found him on top of me, kissing me. That's when I screamed."

"What a creep. Who the fuck does that to get a girl back? I've already changed the codes and organized security to come back tomorrow to fit more cameras. You don't have to worry, Lourde." He paused. "I'm sorry he got to you," he said, and a flicker of regret flashed across his face before disappearing. *Was he still talking about Hunter or someone else?*

"It's not your fault, Barrett." I let the blanket fall around my waist. My shivering had stopped, and Barrett's godlike skin warmed my arms. My gaze dropped to his navy sweats as I breathed in his manly scent.

From his height, he gazed down at me. Then, his softened stare darkened into something that hit me between the thighs.

"What were you dreaming about?"

I dug my teeth into my bottom lip. My heart pounded in my chest—the moment of truth, Lourde. Confess to your brother's best friend your dream was about him or lie.

Screw it.

"I was dreaming it was you who was kissing me."

He sucked in a lungful of air, his dark gaze unmoving. "Fuck, Lourde, don't tell me that." He rubbed his temples.

"Why not?"

His hand gripped the edge of the bed. "You know why."

"I do."

He got up. "No, please don't go," I said, pulling on his wrist.

He turned around. "Will you stay with me tonight? After what happened, I just can't be alone."

He looked at me, weighing my request. "We can stay in my room, and I can sleep on the daybed."

"No, please, stay here?" I was already climbing to my side of the bed, hoping he'd follow.

"Okay, Lourde, just because of what happened tonight. No funny business."

"Funny business?" I smirked at the term, my heart rate spiking off the charts. "Does anyone say that anymore?"

He climbed under the sheets, and his head hit the pillow. Turning to me, he said, "Obviously not."

I rolled my lips together as silence fell between us. His gaze fell to my mouth, and at that moment, I could swear he wanted me.

"Good night, Lourde," he said, rolling toward his side, giving me his back, putting distance between us.

Well, fuck.

11

BARRETT

I woke up with a Texas hard-on and Lourde's head nuzzled in the crook of my neck. Her delicious tits dug into my side, and her arm splayed across my bare chest. With each slow breath she took, she warmed my skin. I wanted nothing more than to wake her up—my head between her legs and the sound of her moaning. The more I stared at her, the less I trusted myself. I slid away quietly and stood at the edge of the bed. She groaned, letting out a light snore as she rolled over, her little shorts revealing the cheek of her ass. My teeth dug into my lower lip at the sight, and the metallic taste of blood lingered on my tongue. *Get the fuck out, Barrett.* Distance and physical exhaustion were needed to curb the temptation.

I returned from a punishing run when I found her making pancakes in my fucking kitchen. Christ, that's two mornings now she'd made breakfast. No woman was ever around long enough to make me breakfast. And I wasn't even fucking her.

"Morning." She tossed me a genuine smile, then turned

the stove off. She wore her hair up in a loose bun. A few strands fell around her heart-shaped face.

I sucked back an entire bottle of Evian, then tossed it in the trash. "Morning."

"This is for last night," she said, stacking the pancakes onto a plate.

"Are you trying to make me lose my muscle mass in a week?" I asked, the smell of pancakes and bacon making me salivate.

I had to admit, waking up next to Lourde had put me in a great mood. I couldn't wash away her scent of apples and berries. I didn't want to. But fuck it, it wasn't rocket science. We were bad news for each other, and I couldn't go there.

Last night she tempted me, but restraint won over. My head and my smarts were always first. Thank fuck she wasn't wearing those pajamas in the kitchen. That restraint was only holding on by a thread. It would likely break faced with the outline of her nipples or curve of her ass in her satin shorts.

She rolled her lips in while dragging her gaze to my sweaty t-shirt. "Unlikely," she muttered.

"I need to take a shower. I stink," I said, pulling my shirt that clung to my chest. Summer in the Hamptons was brutally hot. But it wasn't the heat. I had also pushed myself further this morning. Punishing myself for thinking I could ever have a woman like Lourde.

"You can't eat cold pancakes!" She sat on the stool next to me. "Besides, I like your smell."

Surprised, I turned to her, but she didn't meet my gaze. Instead, she had the bottle of Canadian maple syrup, pouring it on thick, its sticky goo dripping down the stack.

She turned to me, handing me the bottle. "What's wrong with a little naughty treat now and then?" A dare lay behind those hazel eyes, and I knew she wasn't talking about the maple syrup.

"No treats for me." I glared at her, then picked up a fork and shoveled the bacon in my mouth, deciding to limit conversation.

"You're quiet." Dragging her eyes down to the 'V' of sweat down the front of my soaked shirt, she pushed her empty plate to the side.

The truth was, I felt guilty about Hunter finding his way in, and it hadn't left me, and worse, it had stirred up my past. Her ex was a creep. He scared her, but he wasn't dark enough to hurt her. I knew that darkness. Seeing him forcibly on her had me remembering the time I found Dad pinning Mom down against her will. Except on that fateful day, I couldn't ignore it. I'd returned with Dad's gun, the same one he'd threatened my sister and me with for years. I screamed at him to get off her. But he launched at me, and we fought. The gun fired in the scuffle and sent a bullet into Evelyn's leg, then another straight into Mom's chest. She didn't stand a chance.

"There's nothing wrong with quiet."

"Right."

"You didn't need to do this," I said, referring to the stack of pancakes in front of me.

"I did. If it wasn't for you last night, I don't know if I'd have gone back to sleep."

"Well, fuck, that's not what you want a girl to say to you."

She laughed, and it hit me between the temples. "You know what I mean."

"So what are you doing here in the Hamptons, Barrett? Shouldn't you be back in Manhattan?"

"Hopefully, buying another hotel," I said, taking a bite of my semi-warm pancake.

"Oh, is that all?" She smiled, the reflection of the ocean in her eyes. "Why, hopefully?"

"Because the guy's a stubborn jerk and pulling some last-minute deal breakers."

"Oh, anything I can help with?"

I side-eyed her. "No."

"You know I went to the best school, top of my class too. I have a brain and want to use it."

"So, who's stopping you?" *Oh, right.*

She put down her coffee.

"Connor." I nodded. "And your mom."

"Exactly! I have to date the people they want me to date, and I can't work because none of the Diamond women ever worked." She put her head in her hands, letting out a sigh.

"Maybe you can change that. None of the Diamond women are you, Lourde."

It was true. She was different, so different from her mother, who, although lovely, was a true socialite. And I'd even met her grandmother before she passed at a handful of family events. Same as her daughter. Maybe it was the different generation or strong personality, but Lourde was a turtle wanting to hatch and make her own way to the water.

"I've tried, Barrett."

I shook my head. "You haven't tried."

"What?" She narrowed her eyes.

"What have you done? Cried and whined a few times to Mommy? All I'm saying is maybe try something different." The rise and fall of her chest were rapid, her jaw set. I stared at her, taking way too long to pull my gaze away. But when I did, I was the first to break the stare.

She stood up, hitting the underside of the bench with the stool, and took a few steps away. I'd pissed her off. The woman had last night's ordeal to deal with, and I'd gone and been an asshole again. But she deserved the truth.

I stood. "Hey, Lourde, wait."

What are you doing? Let her go, Barrett.

"Try something different?" She stepped toward me, so she was less than an inch from me. "Like this?"

Her hand traced the underside of my shirt. Her smooth hand rode each curve of my muscles and sparked a fire in my belly. I let her get to my pecs before I could muster enough strength to stop her. Roughly, I grabbed her hip with one hand and her wrist with the other. "What are you doing, Lourde?"

"Something different," she said, her voice thick with the hard-on that was forming in my pants.

"Don't play with fire."

Her eyes darkened. Fuck, if it weren't for her brother, I'd bend her over and fuck her right here on my counter. Get her out of my system and move on.

"Why?" she asked, and her other hand trailed her fingers along my mouth. With one hand, I cupped her face. Her lips turned kissable to the force.

"I'm warning you, dollface, *don't.*"

My hand dug into her hip while the weight of her thighs pushed into me.

"I bet you like it rough," she said, sending my pulse to fucking Pluto. Who was this vixen, and where was the proper socialite?

"No one would ever fuck you like I would. But I promise you something. We'll never, ever go there. Your pussy's not worth the trouble."

She gasped, breaking the spell she had over me. I dropped my hand from her hip and the hand that cradled her jaw.

"Now, I'm late for work," I said, like the asshole I truly was.

I knew no one had ever spoken to Lourde like that. I also knew I had to say it in order for her to get over the silly crush she'd always had on me. Hurt her. That was the way to make her forget about me and the stupid infatuation. Now all I had to do was erase her blistering touch on my skin and tell my cock to forget about Lourde Diamond.

12

LOURDE

Over lunch, I filled Pepper and Grace in on Hunters' scary late-night visit, leaving out the part where Barrett slept in my bed. Horrified at the lows he went to get me back, they soon had me convinced to go out tonight and forget about him once and for all.

Except my mind wasn't on my ex. It was on the smooth, curved wall of muscles underneath Barrett's shirt and the sweaty man smell that hit me between the legs.

Your pussy's not worth the trouble. His words swirled in my head. The way the word 'pussy' rolled off his tongue lingered between my thighs. Did I need to be carved from gold for him to want me?

He let my hands wander up his shirt longer than I thought possible. *Did that mean he enjoyed it?* And the way his fingers dug into the shell of my hip—possessive and strong—felt like he wanted to do dirty, unimaginable things to me.

Sure, my brother was a problem, and we'd be hurting him, but that was only if he found out. I needed a rebound. And Barrett, with his towering physique and dark, mysterious eyes, could be it. Heck, I needed him to be it.

Tonight, I chose another skimpy outfit picked out today with the girls on another shopping trip. Because Barrett said I shouldn't wear things like that, I went and bought more. And because he wasn't home when I left, I got away with it.

Thanks to grueling spin classes, my creamy-toned legs looked fucking hot in a short sherbet pink dress with a plunging neckline. Cinched at the waist and braless, it left very little to the imagination.

* * *

"You shouldn't be sitting here with us, especially looking like fire," Pepper said.

She and Grace were happily chilling with their wines in the club's corner. Jake and Dane had set off to the bar to get another round, and Rex, a guy I'd met earlier, had gone with them.

"I'm warming up." I smiled, sipping on a glass of rosé and people watching. "Plus, I've already met Rex."

Lined with sweaty bodies, the club was the most exclusive in town. Thumping bass roared through the speakers, and from upstairs, we watched the DJ below spinning tunes that made the dance floor come alive.

"Why limit yourself to one man," Grace added, dancing in her chair.

"Look, over there. He's a hotty!"

"Who's a hotty?" A familiar voice boomed behind me. *Holy Shit.*

"Barrett?" Pepper lifted her gaze above me.

I turned around. My sight was level with his groin as he

stood directly behind me. I blushed, imagining what it would feel like looking up from on my knees, pleasuring him from here. Wearing dark jeans, a V-neck t-shirt, and sneakers, casual Barrett was alarmingly hot. "Pepper, Grace." He smiled.

His gaze fell to me, directly down the swell of my cleavage. I held my breath as his gaze moved lower to my thighs. "Lourde," he said, his eyes meeting mine. I bit down on my lip like I was in trouble. Fuck, I wasn't a kid.

"What are you doing here?" I straightened my back, and his eyes shot back down to my open neckline.

He blinked, then added, "Your brother sent me this." He turned his phone around, and the screen lit up. A picture of me talking to Rex, the guy I'd met earlier, appeared on his phone. Except I didn't notice his hand was on my ass. I didn't even feel it there if I were honest. *Goddammit.* Okay, so it didn't look good even though it was completely innocent, from my side anyway.

Pepper and Grace leaned over my shoulder to get a shot at the phone. "Oh, that's Rex Fisher," Pepper said. "I think he fancies our Lourde here. He should be back soon."

I glared at her. And she stared back at me a second before the lightbulb went off.

"Ah, Grace and I are going to do a lap, find our men and drag them onto the dance floor."

"Huh?" Grace said, looking at Pepper, then me. Then the penny dropped. "Yes, the boys. Dancing."

I rolled my eyes as Grace quickly shot up and disappeared.

Barrett sat in the seat opposite me, and I crossed my long legs in front of him momentarily, contemplating a Sharon Stone *Basic Instinct* style moment before realizing I was actually wearing a thong.

Whoa! I loved this new me. Confident as hell and embracing my sexuality like never before.

"How did you find me, Barrett?" I asked, cooling my jets.

"It's easy in a small town like this, where social media gives away every location."

"So what, my brother sent you to babysit me?"

"Something like that."

"I can do what I want." I downed the rest of the rosé in a show of defiance.

"Lourde, who's your friend?" Rex appeared by my side, carrying another bottle of champagne, even though I had declined. Yet, here he stood with a bottle of Chandon.

Barrett turned to him like a picture in slow motion. A wry grin spread across his tanned face.

Was this amusing to him?

"This is Barrett. Barrett, meet Rex," I said through gritted teeth.

"Hey, Barrett, I'd shake your hand, but as you can see…" He held up the bottle and two glasses. *Did he not get glasses for Pepper and Grace?*

"So, how do you two know each other?" Rex asked, dragging a chair and sitting beside me.

This should be interesting.

"Barrett is just my brother's friend," I said, placing my hand on Rex's knee.

Barrett's eyes darkened, but he remained still.

"Are you here for the summer, Barrett?" Rex put his arm around my waist, pulling me closer to him. Barrett's jaw twitched, his body becoming rigid.

"No, Rex. We have to go, Lourde. Now. Say goodbye to Rex."

"Wha—" Before I knew it, he'd pulled me upright. Rex's hand slipped from my waist. *Phew, what a relief.*

"Hey, what the hell?" Rex questioned, but Barrett had already grabbed my purse, and with the other hand was now leading me, or rather, dragging me, through the crowd of people toward the exit.

"Stop it, Barrett, this is insane," I said, but like a straight line, he didn't deviate.

His huge hand clasped firmly around mine, tightening hard around my wrist. If I wasn't so irate, I might have liked it.

"Why are you doing this? I'm not a child," I yelled, causing a few people to turn around momentarily.

"At least let me say goodbye to Pepper and Grace!" I looked around, trying to find them in the dark crowd. But he only pulled me harder as we sidestepped the people on the staircase.

"Stop it, Barrett, you're hurting me!" I said, awash with sadness.

He stopped and turned, loosening his grip. Except he was the one who looked in pain—his brows knitted together, his lips in a straight line.

"I'm sorry I hurt you. But you just make me so…" He trailed off, not finishing the sentence. "Just come on."

He turned around and, more gently this time, led me downstairs and out of the club. His Aston Martin took up the sidewalk, half blocking the entrance and the queues of people waiting to get into the club.

"Jesus, Barrett, care much?"

He looked at me, to the car, and the ensuing parking jam. "I don't give a fuck. Now get in."

The five-minute ride back to his home was in silence. I was full of rage. So out of control, I had to distract myself.

I fired off a quick text to the girls in our group chat, explaining that Barrett extracted me from the party like a fucking Navy Seal. All because of a photo Connor sent him. Joking, I said, *send out an SOS.* But part of me wasn't joking. Was this really a message from my brother, and if so, why the fuck couldn't I be at a party with a strange guy?

As soon as we got home, he threw his keys on the table and shouldered out of his jacket.

Taking them one by one, I trudged up the stairs, my body a simmering rage. I walked into my room and slammed the door shut.

Even though I knew I should be thankful for a place to stay, this was too much. I lowered my head in my hands. *Ugh!* My chest tightened, I was so frustrated, and all I wanted to do was scream. The castle I was in had its captor, and I was done for.

Not if I could help it. I slid my phone out of my clutch and dialed my brother.

Pick up!

"Sis, can you stop calling me so late? I'm trying to run the Diamond business."

"Don't you call me sis after the stunt you pulled tonight."

He paused. "What did you expect me to do? That photo was already syndicated in our press rooms before I stepped in and put a stop to it."

"I was just talking to a guy at a party, Connor!"

"Well, with his hand on your ass and you wearing that outfit, one could conclude otherwise. And by one, I mean, the whole fucking nation. You're meant to be with your ex, remember? That story hasn't even broken yet, and you're being photographed with someone else. You're lucky Mom didn't see this. It would ruin the next guy she has lined up for you. He's Mr. Right, by the way."

"Mr. Right? Are you listening to yourself? I love you, brother, but right now, you're a major pain in my ass. Do you know Barrett dragged me from that club? I couldn't even say goodbye to Pepper and Grace. I'm being treated like a child," I yelled.

"I know it seems tough, sis, but know it's for your own good. Please. You can still have a good time this summer. I have to run. My phone's running hot. I think something's just come in."

"Wait—" But he'd already hung up. I threw the phone onto the bed.

I heard Barrett come up the stairs, and quickly I moved, swinging the door open. "You're just like my brother. Both assholes."

He stalked toward me like a predator watching its prey, and my heart thudded louder and louder. His eyes darkened. I couldn't tell if he wanted to wrap his hands around my neck or do inappropriate dirty things to me. I swear, right now, I'd take both options if it meant his hands were on my body. He walked up to me, too close I had to take a step back into my room.

"Now, is that any way to treat the man putting a roof over your head?" His voice was deadly calm, sending goosebumps all over my skin.

I blinked. Barrett regarded me, his prickly stare slowly lowering from my lips, holding on my exposed cleavage, then back up to my eyes.

I swear my heart beat louder than the roar of the ocean. Turning around, I walked inside my room. I couldn't bear for him to see me this vulnerable, this utterly attracted to him. After all, I was so mad at him. So damn mad and frustrated.

His footsteps sounded behind me, and when I turned around, he was in my room. "This isn't fair, Barrett. You know it, and I know it."

He leaned against the wall, his leg crossed over, casually

upright and devilishly wicked. I sat down on the bed, peeling my stilettos off.

"Life's not fair, dollface." Dollface? *Why did I want him to call me that again?*

"Why do you have different rules? You, my brother? Why can't I have fun?"

"I think you're forgetting how lucky you are."

I shot up and walked right up to him. He lowered his gaze to my exposed chest, then back up to me.

"Lucky? I'm a caged animal."

"What is it you want, Lourde?"

"I want…" I drank in his darkened eyes. His gaze made me slightly unbalanced. "I want to be free and single. Have sex with whoever I want, whenever I want."

He laughed, his tone devilish.

"If you're aroused, we can fix that."

"We?" My voice came out husky and dry. *Holy shit, was he thinking what I was thinking?*

He turned me around, so my back was against the wall. It's cold wallpaper sending a shiver up my spine. I swallowed down the lump in my throat. His hand found mine, and I closed my eyes.

Kiss me, fuck me, nail me to the goddamn wall.

With his hand on mine, he controlled my movement, gliding my hand up the inside of my thigh, higher, so he was now underneath the hem of my dress.

I opened my eyes. "What are you doing?" I asked breathlessly.

"Touch yourself, Lourde."

My hand stilled in his. "What?" I half laughed with the thickness in my throat. It was difficult to let out a full laugh. But as his eyes hooded and his breath on my face, I knew he wasn't joking.

"I'll help you, just this once," he choked out. Maybe it

wasn't just me feeling something lodged in my throat.

He pushed my hand further, so it touched me *there*. I gasped. Fuck, this was hot. Dangerous too. I pushed the piece of lace with the force of his hand and slid my index finger to my clit. My breath shortened. I was so wet, so ready, but not for this.

"Rub yourself, dollface."

He shifted his hand, moving it away. I clawed at him with my fingers, keeping his hand firmly on mine. He stilled momentarily. Then, in a circular motion, I started rubbing myself slowly. I tilted my neck, imagining his rough mouth tracing kisses on it. The only thing separating his touch from me was my hand.

He opened his mouth, his breathing labored. I closed my eyes, feeling his thickness swell against my thigh. Greedily, he gripped my hand and took control, careful still not to touch me as he guided me faster and faster. I groaned under him. His bruising pressure on my swelling nub was too delicious to savor any longer. I moaned louder, and he pressed his chest into me, pressing my back into the wall. My skin hummed with warmth.

My breath was ragged, and every nerve ending was like fire and ice, bundled to a coil.

"Barrett!" I breathed as my body found its explosion, and I saw stars.

"That's it," he said hoarsely. He removed his hand and pulled down my dress. "Now that's all you have to do for the summer, and you'll be fine."

He paused, then walked toward the door.

Sucking in a breath, I slid down the wall. My legs were barely able to hold me upright. "You're still an asshole," I yelled.

He turned, and a wicked grin spread onto his delicious lips. "I know, dollface."

13

BARRETT

O kay, so a slight mishap. I wasn't thinking when I grabbed Lourde's hand, pushed aside her scrap of underwear, and thrust her hand onto her clit. But she's the one who wouldn't let me remove it. She clawed at my hand, and I then took over her motion, careful not to touch her but wanting to show her what real pleasure was. The blush on the tips of her cheeks and her moaning only made my thickness swell harder against her thigh. Moments after, I watched her scream my name. *Fuck!* It was the hottest thing I'd ever seen.

With her eyes shut tight and her ragged breath on my face, I wanted to slam my lips on the column of her neck and tear off her flimsy dress, letting it fall to the floor. My loyalty to her brother kept it in my pants. Otherwise, those delicious lips would be wrapped around my hard cock, giving me the release I desperately needed. I had to split a second later and take a cold shower. With my dick in hand, the image of her coming against the wall, I came like a fucking tidal wave.

* * *

I didn't need to go back to Manhattan urgently, but when my multi-story development in Soho had a slight issue, I took it as an opportunity to put some space between Lourde and me, taking the chopper before she woke up this morning.

Leaving it up to my Construction Manager, Joe, to sort out was possible, but that meant I'd needed to face Lourde. We'd had code violations before, and Joe had dealt with them. This one wasn't any different. I'd sorted it in half the time it would've taken Joe. But that wasn't Joe's fault. When Barrett Black called a meeting, it was to get shit done. Heading to the city council meeting with my team of lawyers and architects, we were a show of force, dwarfing the three councilors. And five hours later, the problem was solved.

As the sun lowered its shadow over the city that never sleeps, I had two choices. Go back to the Hamptons tonight or grab a rare ribeye from Benjamins and fly back tomorrow. Again, my head won over, and as I pushed open the door entering Benjamin's steakhouse, a familiar face greeted me.

"Mr. Black, welcome back, sir."

"Harry, nice to see you again."

"Thank you, sir, I have your table available, or will you be joining your friends this evening?"

"Friends?" I scanned the dimly lit room. Benjamins was the best steakhouse in Manhattan, and midweek, it was packed with businessmen and socialites on the prowl. I couldn't see any friends of mine here.

"Mr. Diamond is here with some other guests. Shall I take you to his table?"

Connor's here? A sudden unease came over me.

98

"Sure, I'll say a quick hello." Seeing Lourde's brother after I helped her orgasm wasn't on top of my list of things to do today. Plus, he was likely to be in a meeting. Recently, he'd been working around the clock. There was talk that his dad might step down soon as the president of Diamond Incorporated, and they had been grooming Connor to take his place.

Harry led me along the tiled marble floors and high vaulted ceilings and past the red leather cushioned round booths and table of stunning women.

"Barrett."

I stopped and turned. A familiar face smiled up at me from a table full of women.

"Claudette, hello." She smiled, and the chatter at the table went silent. *Don't flatter yourself.* I never forget a name, even if it was one lousy night. "Ladies, good evening."

She stood up and stalked toward me. Her hair primmed, her face perfectly made up. I heard Harry step away. *Fuck. Don't go, Harry.*

"Don't you look handsome? Charcoal is definitely your color." She grabbed the lapel of my jacket, her manicured fingernails running over it. "They match those dark eyes of yours," she purred.

"How have you been, Claudette?"

"Still thinking about that night," she whispered.

I smiled. "Is that right?" *I'm not.*

"Want to join us?"

"Can't."

She pouted.

"Can we meet up after?"

Desperate wasn't my style, and her body language reeked of it.

"Off to the Hamptons. Another time, though." I

glanced sideways, an invitation for Harry to come the fuck back. Quickly, he appeared at my side.

"Oh. Another time then." She pursed her lips shut.

I smiled.

"This way, sir."

Thank fuck.

Harry ushered me through the dining room. The table they always left open for me sat vacant in the corner near the back. Hidden, just the way I liked it.

I heard Aris' loud laugh and Connor's metallic voice before I saw them. So he wasn't in a meeting after all.

I rounded the corner. Ari and Connor were laughing, and Magnus was there too. I almost had to do a double-take. His hair was ruffled, his eyes were puffy, and he was wearing a t-shirt that could pass as activewear. I'm surprised they even let him in here looking like that.

"What the hell are you doing here?" Ari asked.

"You're all here," I said, slightly relieved to see the boys after everything that was going on.

"Will you be joining Mr. Diamond and his guests, Mr. Black?" Harry asked.

"Damn straight, pull him up a chair, Harry, would you?" Connor asked.

I took the chair from Harry and sat down. Shortly, Harry returned with cutlery and a place setting to set my place at the table.

"So, what are you doing here?" Ari echoed his previous question.

"I had to come back and deal with a problem in Soho." Partly true anyway.

"What are you all doing here? Shouldn't you be with Leila, Magnus? Connor, killing it at work and Ari… what is it you do again?"

They all laughed, except Ari. I shrugged.

"He's going through a rough patch with the missus." Connor slapped Magnus on the back.

Magnus threw back a tumbler of liquid amber. "Caught her screwing the plumber."

I laughed, but when all three sets of eyes glared at me, I knew this wasn't a joke with a punchline. "Oh, shit, you're not kidding." Magnus shook his head.

Magnus married an ex beauty-pageant winner. Really, what did he expect? It had only been a few months since their lavish wedding at a manor in Santa Barbara of all places.

"Sorry, Mag. What now?"

"She flew back to Cali yesterday." He shrugged. "I don't know. Guess I better lawyer up."

"Fucking oath," Connor said. "Anyway, how's the other troublemaker?"

Jesus, I needed a drink before I could answer that one.

"Who?" Ari asked.

"Lourde." Connor deadpanned.

"Fine." Short and sweet, the best way to answer anything about Lourde.

"What can I get you, Mr. Black? Your friends have already ordered."

"Rare ribeye, side of greens, and truffle mash. And a Peroni."

"Of course, sir."

The waiter retreated.

"Why is he asking you about Lourde?" Ari questioned. Out of all the boys, it was Ari and I that clicked immediately. Connor and I started as a business relationship, but as soon as he introduced me to Ari, he was like the long-lost brother I never had. I didn't know if it was because he was the most down-to-earth guy in the group but still loaded from late grandmother's fashion house fortune. Or because he just treated me like he did Connor and Magnus, even though I didn't have a trust fund to fall back on. Sometimes, with Magnus and Connor, I got the feeling I was still inferior, all because I was new money rather than old money.

"Hunter cheated on Lourde, so she's single and in the Hamptons."

"She has some serious bad luck with men." Ari shook his head.

"Maybe one of us should show her that the older men are where it's at." Magnus laughed, knowing exactly what reaction he was going to get.

"Not funny, cocksucker. Actually, she's meant to have a babysitter, and he's fucking here."

"I'm no babysitter, Connor," I snapped.

"Jesus, settle down. I didn't mean it like that."

"I'm going back tonight. Pipe the fuck down." *Where the heck did that come from?* Guess I am now.

"Fuck, let me call her. She better not be wearing that scrap of material she had on yesterday."

Connor slid out his phone and stood up, pacing to the nearby steel windows.

"So you got your eye on her, then?" Ari asked, a slight smirk spreading onto his lips.

"I don't know why. She's a big girl." I took a long swig of my Peroni.

"Just don't get any ideas. She's a honey pot, but he's a fucking wasp," Magnus chewed out, pointing to Connor.

"No ideas from me. I hardly see her anyway. I'm at work, and she's usually out when I get home."

"So, she's living with you?" Ari questioned, a little too hyped.

Dammit, would he just quit it already? "Hunter fucked her

over, remember? They're all staying at a place for the summer he arranged. Connor asked me to take her in."

"Ooh boy. I wonder if the delicate angel will break the dark playboy of Manhattan."

"Many have tried and not succeeded," Magnus added.

"Not interested." I gulped my beer back.

"Yeah, but she is. Hasn't she always had this crush on you? I see the way she looks at you. You're the mysterious one. The bad boy everyone wants to dabble in before they settle for Mr. Responsible from a good family," Ari said.

A good family. Fuck, I didn't come from the sort. From *their* sort. My family was gone. My sister was all who remained before my father, El Diablo himself, could take her too.

It was the sight of my mother, lying lifeless, that haunted me—every damn day. The bullet that was meant for him, pierced her heart. And it killed her instantly. I killed my mother. Dad pulled the trigger in a fight, but I held the gun in my hand. The state ruled it an accident. A terrible accident. An act of self-defense against an abusive father and husband. But it was my mother lying on the floor not him. And her screams have haunted me every day since.

"Stop daydreaming about Lourde's panties, Barrett." Magnus laughed.

At the same time, Connor returned to the table. *Great.*

"What the fuck?" Connor rubber-banded his head, his gaze piercing mine.

"He was kidding, Connor," Ari joked. Connor's scowl replaced the looped, lifeless image of my mother in my arms.

"Barrett isn't interested one iota in your sister. In fact, he was just saying how much he loathed babysitting her." Ari nodded toward me. His look as stern as Connors. A friendly warning, no doubt. I nodded. Nothing going on. I haven't touched her. *Technically.*

"Everything all right?" I looked up at Connor. My curiosity got the better of me, and I wondered if she was heading to another party tonight.

"She assures me she's fine. She checked into the Inn with the girls and their boyfriends. Then going back home."

"No party then?" A relief came over me.

"You sure seem interested in someone who's not meant to be." Magnus grinned.

"Shut the fuck up. What are you trying to do here?" I glared at him. I didn't care if he just caught his wife screwing around. He was skirting on landing a punch to the face if he wasn't careful.

"He wouldn't fucking dare touch her." Connor glared at me.

"It goes without saying." *Fuck.*

Connor threw back his whiskey. "No party. She's still livid with you for dragging her away. Who needs to hire muscle when your bestie can do it for you?"

The steak was bloody and delicious. The boys sank back a few top-shelf whiskeys and were discussing Magnus' impending decision with his cheating wife taking half his fortune. Yes, the dickwad's prenup was rather generous.

It was after ten o'clock when I'd decided I should head back to the Hamptons. I had an early meeting, and the last whiskey had me feeling rather relaxed.

"Hey, I'll walk you out. I'm heading off too," Ari said. "I've got Estella, my late-night fuck waiting back at my apartment.

"Christ, about time you got more pussy than me." Heads turned, but I didn't give a fuck as we walked past late-night diners toward the exit.

"Don't I always?" Ari winked.

"Keep dreaming, Ari."

"There will be no sleeping tonight. Estella's a goddamn nymph!"

My car waited for me out front, but Ari pulled me to the side before I got in.

"What's the main reason you're following me out? Let me guess…"

"Don't fuck her," he said, a warning in his tone.

"Guessed right."

"You want to, don't you?" Ari's eyes were wide.

Maybe. "No."

"Fuck, why do I feel I'm already too late, Barrett?"

"Ari, you've had too much to drink. Go home, get laid."

He narrowed his eyes at his best attempt at another warning. But fuck him, fuck all of them. I'd never listened to anyone before, and I wouldn't start now. I wasn't touching Lourde, but that was because she deserved better. As damn hard as she made it around me, I knew my limits. I was in control, and she was my best friend's little sister.

Besides, she deserved way better than a monster like me.

14

LOURDE

Another day and evening went by when Barrett wasn't at home.

He hadn't even told me he'd gone back to Manhattan. I had to hear that from my brother when he phoned me, shooting me another warning, "Wear something that slutty again, and I'll get my driver to pick you up and drag you back home."

My evening with the girls and their boyfriends was okay, apart from feeling like the single loser friend.

I'd had a taste of danger and excitement, and I craved more. More of his hand high on my thigh, taking control of my clit. His warm breath brushing my cheek and his blistering touch on my skin. But all I felt was my touch. It was pure torture that he couldn't or wouldn't touch me. He watched as I got myself off. When I reopened my eyes, he was staring at me. His dark eyes heated, his enormous erection pressed into my thigh. I wanted him to throw me against the wall and put that hard dick inside of me. I'd never wanted anything so much in my entire life.

And I was going to have it. If just once. I needed to

taste the sweet dirty nectar that Barrett was. There was no way I'd tell my brother. There's no way he would either. The problem was, he was too loyal. He wouldn't dare ruin a friendship just for a one-time pussy, as he called it.

I turned and felt for the nightstand, flicking the lamp on as I sat up in bed.

I thrashed about. Even trying to read, but nothing was working. I'd heard Barrett come home an hour ago, but it was after midnight, and he was still downstairs banging about, louder than a tiger in a cage, sounding angry, so I let him be.

But how was I supposed to sleep with that going on? I tossed off the duvet. "Enough."

Running my fingers through my hair, I trudged down the stairs, pausing at the last step.

Barrett had flicked through all the books on the floor. His bookshelf was a twisted mess.

"You just about done?" I asked, throwing my hand to my hip.

He turned around and took me in. Bare-faced and likely tired bags, I was wearing my satin camisole and little shorts.

"I didn't realize it was your house?" He grinned, then turned back around to the mess he'd created on the over-sized Turkish floor rug.

I walked into the living room, now blocking him from his precious books. "It's not, but if I knew you'd be reno-vating, I'd have looked elsewhere."

"Elsewhere?" He dropped the books.

"Why didn't you tell me you were heading back to the city."

"Why, were you worried, dollface?"

A tingle shot between my legs.

"More annoyed."

"What do you want, dollface?"

"I… I…" My words were failing me.

"Do you want to scream my name when you come?"

Jesus Christ, if he wanted me to feel embarrassed, well, maybe I was a little, but I wouldn't give him the satisfaction of knowing that.

"Yours or anyone else's."

His eyes darkened. He pulled his arm around my waist and pulled me closer. He ran his hand down my body, and shivers shot up my spine. Fuck, I wanted him so badly.

"There will be no one else's, Lourde," he said, snapping his fingers off my body in an instant. He let me go so quickly I nearly fell back and toppled over his fallen books.

"You're an asshole, tease," I said, sullen and broken from his near touch.

He grinned. "Haven't we been through this asshole thing? But tease? You think I'm a tease?"

I smelled liquor on his breath. Now was a better time than any to get him to want me and break his loyalty to my brother. I stepped forward and ran my fingers down his neck. He shifted his neck to the side, his gaze lowering to mine. He reached up and grabbed my hand, lowering it down past my breasts to the waistline of my shorts.

"You're a bad girl, Lourde."

"Only when you're around."

I grabbed his hand and lowered it between my legs. He had his hand clasped to mine, careful not to touch me there. I ached for his hands, his touch directly on my skin, but he didn't. He inhaled sharply as his hand searched for underwear but didn't find any. He moved for me, taking control of my hand as it circled my nub.

The moonlight hit his face. I drank him in as I became wetter and hotter by the sensations taking over my body.

Dark eyes drank in my soul. I tried to kiss him, but he pulled away. He moved my hand faster.

"Touch me, Barrett," I whispered.

"No, dollface." His voice was raspy and hoarse.

I groaned as he played with me. "Don't make me beg."

Suddenly, he stopped the motion of my hand, just when I was so close too. *Fuck no!*

"Stay still." With one hand, he slid my shorts off completely, leaving me exposed in front of him. He kneeled in front of me, smelling me between my thighs.

He groaned. "No one ever calls me a tease and gets away with it."

The next thing I knew, he'd plunged his tongue deep inside my folds. *Holy fuck.* I threw my head back. The sensation was fucking mind-blowing. My skin was lava hot as he stroked me deeper and deeper with his tongue, taking my clit and circling it like a windmill. I groaned, the air disappearing from my lungs.

"You taste delicious, dollface."

I groaned again—my legs like jelly, my heart rate to oblivion. I looked down, but I wasn't dreaming. Barrett was between my legs, fucking me with his delicious tongue.

"I've wanted to fuck you with my tongue for too long," he said, and his dirty words tipped me to the edge.

I shoved his head back between my thighs. I felt him smirk against me, then dip his tongue into my slit. This time he fucked me hard, his tongue darting in and out, then his fingers dipped into me. One, then two, then… *holy shit.*

Before I could comprehend what was happening, my body coiled and tossed. I squeezed his head into me, absorbing everything he had. I shut my eyes, going to la-la land.

Breathing hard, I tried to refill the air lost in my lungs

and regain any semblance of a normal breath. Any harder, and the concierge doctor might have to pay a visit.

He got up, sliding my satin shorts back up my thighs as he did. Standing in front of me, his lips glistened. I was on his lips, and it was the hottest thing I'd ever seen. I reached for his belt, but he put his hand out, stopping me. "Let me return the favor."

Staring down at the tent in his pants, I rolled my lips inward.

"As much as I want those bow lips on my cock, I think we've crossed the line enough tonight, don't you?"

I pouted. There wasn't anything more I wanted right now than to take him. To find out if the rumors about his appendage amongst the socialites were true. To pleasure him the way he just blew my mind.

"What's a bit more going to hurt?"

His eyes flashed with something incomprehensible, and he pushed my hand away.

"No, Lourde." His voice boomed.

I blinked, fighting the tears that nearly pricked at my eyes.

Did he regret this? Of course, he did. He hadn't even kissed me, and now I couldn't touch him?

I removed my hand from his belt buckle and glared at him. He glared back. The standoff was going nowhere. He wasn't letting me touch him. Too weak to argue, I steamrolled back upstairs to my room. I heard him groan and hiss, but I didn't care. It was too late for apologies.

* * *

The morning broke after an amazing sleep, but the clear sky and blistering heat did little to make sense of the night before.

Breakfast sucked. My fruit was bland, lacking any sweetness.

He returned from a run, ate his prepared breakfast, and was on the phone pretty much the entire time. I was so confused. *What was this?* And why did I want him to do bad things to me when he was the biggest jerkface of all? He didn't want anyone to touch me. But why?

I hit the plate in the sink louder than normal, just for effect.

"Bad night?"

Finally, he speaks.

"No, not at all." Two could play this game. Although I wasn't entirely sure what game it was we were playing.

"Sorry about last night."

I turned around.

"Which part?" Just to be sure, I asked.

He tilted his head as his gaze dropped to my waist.

"Oh, right." A blush heated my neck, wrapping its way around my shoulders.

"It won't happen again."

What? Why not?

He smirked. "It can't happen again, Lourde." His smirk resolved into a thin line.

But before I could think of anything to say, he got up, grabbed his phone, and walked out. "I'll see you tonight," he said, shutting the front door and leaving me in the hallway, angry as hell.

15

BARRETT

A momentary lapse of judgment had me on my knees tasting her sweet juices, and more than once today, I was distracted. At meetings, I imagined her taste on my tongue or making her come with me inside her, screaming my name.

The warning Ari shot me last night was fruitless. It couldn't happen again. It shouldn't. I had never taken advice from others, except my sister, Evelyn. But with Lourde, I was playing with fire. After one taste of her, she had doused me from head to toe in gasoline, holding the match.

I was her babysitter, her protector, and nothing more. But the way she moaned my name between her peach lips looped in my head, distracting me all day long. Nothing would've given me more of a hard-on than to see Lourde Diamond wrapping those lips around my cock. Models, celebrities, and bored Manhattan housewives couldn't get my dick as hard as she did.

But I slayed women like a bad habit. And Lourde Diamond wasn't a woman to slay. She was delicate with her porcelain skin, small pointy nose, and stiletto legs. The men handpicked by her mother tamed her inner wildness. They were the right men for her. Weren't they?

But since becoming single, Lourde was anything but tame. She wanted more. Craved more.

The devil on my shoulder wove his pitch fork, willing me to yield to her. Fuck her like she's never been fucked before. In doing so, give her a taste of the freedom she deserves before being trapped with another so-called perfect match. But on my other shoulder, a fucking angel had reigned supreme. The white glow of the angel, a blinding reminder her brother would cremate me while my heart was still beating if I gave in.

Distraction was key. With every day that passed in the Hamptons, I was getting closer to securing this once-in-a-lifetime deal. But closing it out to return to my apartment in the Upper West Side wasn't as appealing as it was when I arrived a week ago.

But not yet. There were a few more loose ends my team couldn't do without me, then this hotel in East Hampton would be mine—and for several million less than asking.

Last-minute plans for dinner derailed my plans to see Lourde tonight. I wondered what she was up to. The banter we had back and forth, although damn infuriating sometimes, I craved. But tonight's meeting couldn't wait, and I had to get Tobias here with his research before the night was over.

I sat around the table at the Pond and Pony restaurant, with my president of Legal, Tobias to my right, and Cary and Simon, representing the hotel, opposite.

I peeled at the paint on the armchair, flicking it to the ground. Outdated furnishing, old carpets, chipped boards, and staff who looked like they'd been here longer than the building desperately needed new owners. Soon, I'd get my hands on this outdated hotel and turn it into a new seven-star exclusive Hampton's retreat. Tearing it down and starting again was what I did best. Old furniture, peeling wallpaper, and downright dark and closed spaces weren't worth the cost of restoring the old icon, even if it had some interesting lines and was one of the oldest hotels in the Hamptons.

Tobias talked about the hotel's history with Cary and Simon over barely passable steak tartare and ceviche while I sat in silence, confirming everything in the documents Tobias passed to me before dinner started.

"I know I don't have to tell you this, Barrett, but this hotel has been an icon for decades. I really can't see how you'll get past the uproar of the locals if you tear it down."

I closed the documents, having everything I needed in front of me.

"You definitely shouldn't be saying that." I pushed away the half-eaten plate of food in front of me.

He looked at his other suit like the cat that swallowed the canary. "Why?"

"You're going to give me ten million off asking because no one in their damn mind would buy this run-down hotel in its current state and revamp it. It just costs too much."

Laughter spilled from his lips. "Ten million? You're dreaming, Barrett," Simon said, pushing his plate away and folding his arms over his rounded chest.

"The fact is, Simon, you have no one else interested. The hotel is in the red hundreds of thousands of dollars, and if you don't sell it to me in the next three months, you'll close your doors for good."

"What?" Simon opened his mouth. "How could you possibly know that?"

I cast my eyes down at the document in front of me. Glaring up, Simon did the same.

"What is that?" Cary asked, lowering his wire frames to the bridge of his nose.

"Your figures didn't add up. So I had my team investigate. And what they found was very interesting." I tapped my fingers on the documents. "Tabloid-worthy interesting." A grin stretched from my mouth.

Simon looked at Cary, then back at me. "You know nothing, Barrett. I knew getting into bed with you would be trouble. We're not doing anything of the sort."

"Sure. So do you think the media will be interested to know the board skimmed two million dollars? Or how about this headline, *Hampton Hotel Blames Layoffs on Slow Seasons Instead of Covert Ski Trips in Aspen with the Board's Mistresses.*" I turned to Tobias. "Do you think Connor Diamond over at Diamond Incorporated will want to know that?"

"Maybe we should ask him?" Tobias said, playing along.

I shrugged, sliding my phone out of my suit pocket.

"Jesus Christ, Barrett, stop," Cary yelled.

"You can't do this, Barrett," Simon said, his jaw ticking.

"But I am."

"You, Cary, John, and the other board members made your own bed. I expect my offer to be signed and returned by the end of the week with the discount." Cary threw his napkin across the table.

As well as knowing the names of people I associated with, be it women or businessmen, I always took note of anyone trying to skim me. And these polished men in their late sixties thought their payday was coming. Well, checkmate, fuckers. This hotel was mine.

"I think this meeting has come to its end." Simon pushed out his armchair.

"Pleasure," I said, not bothering to get up and see them off.

"Jesus Christ. They played exactly into your hands, Barrett."

"Like bait. Revise the contract tonight and send it off for their signatures. The sooner we stitch this up, the sooner I can go back to Manhattan."

"Why the rush? It's beautiful out here. When's the last time you had a break?"

"Oh, darling. That's so sweet you care about me like that." I rolled my eyes. "I'll sleep when I'm dead," I said.

"Of course, you will." I followed his gaze to the entrance windows.

A group of gorgeous women passed by, entering the bar attached to the hotel. Black hair. That was Pepper. Copper hair. Wasn't that Grace? Two men walked beside them. I craned my neck to see if anyone was behind them. *What the fuck?*

Dressed in a low-cut dress with a high slit, Lourde was my brand of elixir. Was she doing this to kill me? She hadn't noticed me as she draped her leg over a bar stool, but everyone in this hotel noticed her. She was a single girl and easy prey for predators. She came across as easy. Innocent.

I pushed my chair out. It caught on the carpet. "Excuse me."

"Where are you going? Do you know them, Barrett? Shit, of course, you do," he mumbled.

"Get that contract to them asap, Tobias, and charter the next plane out of here to your pregnant wife."

Whatever he said, I didn't hear. I didn't care. I'd

already left the table, steamrolling toward her like a derailed freight train.

Why was she wearing that after I explicitly said not to? She looked fucking amazing. Sin-worthy, amazing. Couldn't she see she attracted the eyes of all sorts? She couldn't be in the public eye like that. Heck, she was my responsibility. My vein ticked in my neck, and I ran my finger across my jaw between my neck and my collar, loosening it.

Why was I letting her affect me this way? *It was just a dress, Barrett.*

"The sexy grinch is here," Pepper said in a not-so-subtle whisper.

"Pepper, Grace." I smiled. "Lourde." My smile vanished.

She stepped off the bar stool and strutted past me like I wasn't even there. I walked behind her, then pulled at her wrist. "Where are you going?"

She wriggled from my grasp. "It's my turn to pay," she said, walking off and leaving me to watch her pert ass as it swished from side to side.

If she knew I was here, she didn't care.

"Sit down, Barrett." I turned around, and Pepper pointed to an empty stool. "Let me introduce you to my boyfriend, Jake."

Reluctantly, I pulled my gaze away from my elixir and sat down. The last thing I wanted to do was to meet her friends' boyfriends. I'd avoided doing that at my own party. Even when I saw Connor talking with Pepper and him, I'd avoided it.

"Hey, man, great to meet you. I saw your photo in the paper. Did you really just make four hundred million on 21 Park?"

I narrowed my eyes. *Jesus, fuck, who asks that?*

"Jaaake! Don't be so rude!"

"It's okay, Pepper. Something like that, Jake."

"I'm Dane, and can I just say, well the fuck done." I laughed and shook Dane's extended hand.

"Champagne is here," Lourde said, setting down a tray of pale yellow-filled glasses. What was she, the help now?

After Jake toasted to something fucking stupid, I took her to the side and held my face down to her ear. She shuddered suddenly at my closeness. "Just so you know, you're not going anywhere like that, dollface."

"Oh, yes, I am. We're getting a pre-drink here before the party up on Lane Street." She straightened, and her perfume mixed with her defiance made my dick twitch. Why was she defying me like that? And why the fuck did I want to spank that defiance right out of her?

Again, she swatted me away. The others chatted, oblivious to our exchange.

My chest rose and fell. "Don't play with me, Lourde."

"Or what, Barret. What will you do to me?"

She stood at the bar and tilted her head to the side, an inch from me. Her black, sultry cat-like eyes fixed on mine.

I glared at her, a silent plea not to tempt me, and after a beat, she sat back down. If she was daring me, I couldn't bite. I had to stay in control for both of us.

I watched her sip her champagne, laughing, carefree, and happy. Every now and then, she'd catch me doing so. I let her. As I politely engaged in conversation about construction and Manhattan politicians, she handed me a Peroni. How she knew I drank Peroni was a mystery. Regardless, I sipped on it, listening to Jake and Dane name-drop and swing their little dicks around in front of their girlfriends. If it weren't so pathetic, it would've been cute. Plus, it was no skin off my nose.

The girls grabbed their belongings. "So, will you be coming with us, Barrett?" Pepper asked.

I looked at Lourde, and she stared back at me. I couldn't let her go out on her own, could I? *No.*

"For a drink, sure," I said.

"Wicked!" Dane said, walking out with Grace.

"Well, take that damn suit off then and let your hair down," Lourde said, her hands finding their way to my tie.

The others moved outside, and we remained. I let her untie it and undo my top two buttons. Watching her up close, her smooth skin, a hint of blush on her cheeks, long black eyelashes fan out, and her scent of vanilla hit my nostrils. I pushed away the image of fucking her on my bed as quickly as it came.

A few hours later and the party on Lane Street was bursting with people. The best of what the Hamptons had to offer was right here, yet I couldn't give two fucks. I wanted every guy in this place to stop eye-fucking Lourde.

Her friends weren't so bad. Actually, the boys weren't too bad either. They passed the time and distracted me from Lourde's long legs. But right now, more than ever, I needed a distraction. On her way back from the girls' room, she had stopped and was now talking to a guy. A guy who looked pissed and eager for a one-night stand. Just the type she wanted.

"You're very watchful of her, aren't you?" Grace questioned.

"Her brother can't afford the bad press."

"Uh, huh." She sipped her champagne, glaring at me.

"To be honest, I have better things to do, but you guys

are bearable." I grinned, taking my beer to my lips and oddly enjoying myself.

"Gee, thanks. Think of it from her point of view. She's twenty-three and having to be chaperoned to a party because of her name."

"It's tough being born into privilege." I put the beer back down on the table full of empty champagne and beer bottles.

"So, you weren't?"

"Born into privilege?" I scoffed. "No, definitely not."

"What are we talking about over here?" Lourde walked over toward me. Sitting on my lap, she tossed her leg over my thigh, her peachy ass nestled near my groin.

"Are you drunk?" I gripped her hips, rounding her, so she faced me.

"Maybe."

Pepper grinned. "We were talking about Barrett not coming from a privileged upbringing."

"Connor said it's just you and your sister. Yet, you never mention her. Are you so overprotective of her too?"

My leg throbbed. I stood up, and she slid off me toward the floor. I grabbed her before she fell and pulled her upright, her chest slamming into mine. She glared at me. Fear held behind her hazel eyes. Good, she should be afraid of me. "That's enough, Lourde. We're going."

I turned to the others, who were no doubt looking our way now. "Pepper, Grace, fellas, it's been real, but I'm taking this one home."

"Oh right! Have fun, you two." Pepper and Grace jumped up, saying their goodbyes. Grace whispered something in her ear. Lourde giggled, and the noise swirled inside my chest.

* * *

My head hit the pillow, but I couldn't sleep. What Lourde said about my sister infuriated me. But I couldn't get her long legs out of my mind. The way she effortlessly held a crowd's attention without even knowing it. And the curve of her breasts when she was on my lap, I had a bird's-eye view. Containment is a motherfucker, and my dick had been in my pants far too long, especially after tasting her delicious elixir between her legs.

She'd passed out before I could even talk to her and berate her for her carelessness tonight. Drunk at a private party and wearing what she wore were two things ripe for disaster. She was recognizable, and it only took one jerk to go for her. Ruin her perfect image and the Diamond name that was so sacred in America. I promised her brother I'd take care of her. But it was a promise I wasn't sure I could keep.

I helped her upstairs and into bed, changing her into her shorts and camisole. And fuck it, I was only human. I stared at her breasts for way too long. Perfectly natural, creamy skin and soft pink nipples screamed to be sucked on hard. With that image imprinted on my mind, forget sleeping. I'd been lying here for hours.

A faint tap at the door pulled me from my thoughts.

"Barrett, are you awake?"

I sat up and got out of bed. I stared back at the alarm clock. Fuck, it was four in the morning.

"Yes. Are you okay?"

She slid into my room, the moonlight hitting her purple camisole. "I'm fine."

"You seem fine, but you're here at this ungodly hour." Obviously, the haze of alcohol had worn off. I regarded her. She'd washed the makeup off her face and let her hair fall over her shoulders.

"What can I do for you, Ms. Diamond, at four in the

morning?"

"I just wanted to say I'm sorry."

"For what exactly, Lourde?" I turned and paced the length of my room. "For what you wore?"

"No." She shook her head from side to side. "I can wear what I like," she said softly.

"No?" *What the hell?* And why was she so calm? A shot of adrenaline coursed through my veins.

"For talking to random men in front of me?"

She shrugged. "Maybe."

"Then what?"

"For this." She lowered the thin straps of her camisole, and it slid round her waist, exposing her creamy tits.

Fuck! My throat clogged, but I took a deliberate step toward her.

"And this." She slid off her shorts, then her camisole followed, dropping to the floor.

She stood naked, the light shining on her curves, her nipples engorged.

"I want you to do bad things to me, Barrett."

She raked her teeth across her bottom lip, and I felt my dick come alive in my pants.

"I can't touch you, dollface," I said on a breath.

"Can't or won't? I don't want you to just touch me, I want you to ruin me."

Well, fuck.

She pulled me in, so my bare chest hit her warm skin. Her hands slid from around my waist, dipping just below my hips. The tips of her fingers warmed my skin and sent me harder than a boulder. She looked up at me with an innocence I wanted to knock out of her.

With one fling, I pulled my pants down. Lourde gazed down at my hard cock like it was a shrine. Her mouth tipped open, then returned her face to mine.

"You asked for it, dollface."

She pushed off her toes and looked up at me for permission to kiss me.

Only you, Lourde. Otherwise, kissing was off the menu with all women. I devoured her lips, pushing her into my cock as she pressed into me, groaning in my mouth. Her tongue feverishly found mine as our tongues thrashed about in a desperate kiss. Tilting her head back, I traced the column of her neck with bruising kisses. I didn't give a fuck if I left my mark.

I spun us and led her to the bed. Then I pushed her down and climbed on top of her. Instantly, I took my mouth to one breast, then greedily to the next, and raked my teeth between her engorged nipples and grazing down. "Jesus," she hissed the word through her teeth.

"We're only beginning. Soon you'll be begging me to stop."

"No, don't stop," she commanded through heavy breaths.

"Open your legs for me, dollface. I want to see you."

Her eyes widened, but she did as I asked. Her breasts were red from my rough touch and burning kisses. There wasn't anything else I wanted more right now than to take Lourde and fuck her innocence right out of her.

I plunged my long tongue between her legs. She squirmed beneath me, and I placed my hands on her stomach, pinning her down.

"Keep still. I'm going to fuck you with my tongue. Then you're going to beg for my dick inside you."

"Please." She moaned.

I went to work, expertly gliding in and out of her delicious cunt. She moaned deeper, and her breath drew short and sharp as the seconds ticked by. I plunged into her further, and the wetter she got, her juices coated my mouth. I fingered her with two fingers, then three, hitting her spot, and she arched her back, on the edge.

"Fuck," she screamed as she came around my fingers and my tongue circling her nub.

Before she could catch her breath, I needed to fuck her.

I reached for the foil packet in my side drawer and rolled it on. I was so engorged, the damn thing struggled to get on.

"Holy fuck, Barrett, no one has ever—"

"Now turn around, dollface. I'm going to fuck you from behind, and you'll take what I have to give you."

She sat up and wrapped her arms around me, shoving her breasts into my chest and her tongue down my throat. I cupped her ass and pushed her into me as we were both on our knees, tangled in tongues and limbs.

"Disobedient, aren't we?" I clasped her chin, so she pulled away. Kissing Lourde wasn't a good idea. I needed to do to her what she needed me to do. Give her the best fuck of her life.

Her eyes blazed, and a smirk tipped on her lips.

"Oh, you asked for it." I smacked my hands onto her ass, cupping her so that her legs wrapped around me. I leaped up and carried her off the bed. With her legs clawed around my hips, I walked us over to the wall and threw her against it, *hard*. I plunged my tip into her. "Fuck," I growled out on a breath. Her cunt was perfect.

She wrapped her hands around my neck. Without warning, I slammed into her with my full cock, hitting her back wall. "Argh," she moaned. "Fuck me."

Repeatedly, I plunged into her while squeezing her ass against the wall. Heat burned in my chest, and I couldn't help but nip along her jaw to the hollow of her neck, where my teeth sank a bit deeper.

"Barrett!" Her eyes shut, her cheeks fiery red.

"That's it, dollface. Come for me again," I commanded.

"I... I..." Over and over, I plowed into her with my thick cock.

She tilted her head back, and I sucked at her neck, tracing her reddened skin while taking her nipple, squeezing it between my fingers. Pinned against the wall, her body coiled, then released. "Oh, my God." Her cunt throbbed and pulsed around me.

The sounds coming from her tipped me to the edge. Her kisses found my neck, and my body tensed. My balls pulled up, and my dick throbbed inside her. "Fuck me," I roared, my body unfurling around her.

For a few moments, we remained like this. Her legs were still wrapped around me, and her head was draped over my shoulder. Our chests rose and fell, and I could feel her heart beat against my chest.

I lifted her over to my bed and went to clean myself up. When I returned from the bathroom, she lay naked on my pillow, a sheet half up her body.

"I don't do sleepovers, dollface."

When she didn't reply, I sat on the bed, leaning over. Her eyes were closed tight.

"Lourde?"

Now what? I was in unfamiliar territory. I had two choices. I could wake her or slide in next to her and try to sleep a few hours until the sun came up. I pulled the sheet up and over her delicious curves and lithe body, then the blanket. I'd decided without even realizing it. I lay next to her, watching her sleep, the gray shadow highlighting her rogue lips and thick lashes. The rosy glow of her cheeks was still clear from a few moments ago.

I listened to her breathing rise and fall, and not long after, I drifted off to sleep.

16

LOURDE

Like a struck match, his touch lingered and burned on my skin. I felt a warmth between my legs just thinking about it. I realized I wasn't dreaming when I opened my eyes and the ache remained. I traced down to the pleasurable feeling of finding Barrett's finger circling my nipple.

"Morning." I moaned out. "That feels nice."

He tugged at my nipple harder. "Ow!" I said, the pain only lasted a second, but the pleasure lingered.

"I'm not nice, dollface…"

I turned, finding his hooded gaze all over me. Wanting to talk to him about last night was important, but now, with his fingers circling my nipples, I couldn't think straight.

"I've had nice. My exes were nice enough, but nice didn't work out."

I lay on my back as he dropped his hand, trailing the underside of my breasts, then slowly teasing down the column of my stomach. Every nerve ending already lit, fired on all cylinders.

"What do you want?" He groaned.

I arched my back and shut my eyes. "I want more of this."

He chuckled, then stopped his hand from moving lower. "I bet you do."

Breathless and confused, I opened my eyes and turned to him. "No one has to know, Barrett."

"Once we can get away with, but twice?" He shook his head and began to get up.

No, this can't be just once.

"You want me just as much as I want you, Barrett," I blurted.

"I don't want you, Lourde." He flicked the covers off and sat up on the edge of the bed.

I ignored the stabbing pain and the flicker in his eyes. Adrenaline fueled my body as I leaped up. From behind, I wrapped my arms around him and pressed my naked body into his muscly back. Instantly, he gripped my arm, dragging me around and onto his lap.

Now wasn't the time to be self-conscious as I lay naked before him. His eyes burned, anger and lust a deadly combination. One that knocked any self-consciousness out of me and replaced it with a throbbing ache.

Lowering my mouth to his, I said, "I don't believe you." With my free hand, I traced his ripped muscles, toying with the elastic waistband of his pants.

His hand fell around my throat, and I swallowed, staring into his jade eyes. I should be scared, but around him, I wasn't. He lowered his face to mine. "Do you like making me mad?" His voice was gravelly low.

"Yes," I whispered.

He paused. His gaze drifted to my lips. My heart pounded in my ear.

"Fuck it. I'm going straight to hell anyway." His lips

crashed into mine, and I gasped momentarily before desperately seeking his tongue.

Rough. Pure. Carnal. He squeezed my neck slightly, just enough to elicit insane pleasure. I ran my hands through his hair, tugging at the roots. His hand slid round the base my neck, tipping me so my spine curved, spilling my breasts forward.

A groan sounded from the back of his throat, and I knew he wanted this as much as I did. His teeth grazed my nipple. Biting down on it, I moaned in pleasure. His fingers spread me apart. Wasting no time, he dipped two fingers, dragging my wetness to my nub, then back down again.

I squeezed my body, absorbing his touch. "Barrett." I panted.

"I like my name on your lips, dollface."

I like you.

His erection pressed into my thigh. "Take these off," I groaned, fumbling with the waistband of his pants.

"Impatient, are we?" He pushed me down onto the bed. Climbing on top of me, his strong arms pressed to either side of me.

"I'm going to fuck you hard, Lourde." I sucked in a breath. He went to his side drawer and tore the corner of his condom with his teeth, slid his pants down, and let his erection spring free. I sucked my lips in at the sight of his massive engorgement. Fuck, the man was gifted, and I was wetter than hurricane season in Hawaii.

I grinned. "Hurry."

His eyes flared as he finished rolling on the end of his condom.

"Lie on your stomach."

I did as he said. My heart thumped erratically.

A blinding pain erupted on my ass. "Ouch!" Did he just spank me? *Holy fuck.* I throbbed for him.

He dipped his fingers into me quicker this time, and my breath escaped me.

"I'm the asshole, dollface, remember?" He plunged into me from behind, filling me deeply.

"Ah, fuck." He hissed on a breath through gritted teeth.

I gripped the sheets between my fingers, taking everything he had to give me.

Fuck, I didn't know how we fit. He was huge. But somehow, it was perfect. He stretched me with each thrust. Further and further, hitting my spot each time. I was so close. My body heated, and my nipples rubbed against the sheet at every thrust. Barrett grabbed my hair with one hand while his other hand rubbed my ass. He trailed the line of my ass, hovering over my back hole—*oh fuck me.* I pushed my hips up toward his finger.

"You an ass virgin, dollface?"

I swallowed. I didn't have a voice. I could only nod.

"Not anymore." He plunged his finger into me, and I moaned into the sheets.

Holy Fuck. Full. Weird. Amazing. Unspeakable.

He thrust himself into me deeper, his finger massaging my hole. My breath was robbed from me. Was it possible to die from pleasure overload?

"That's it," he groaned. "Come for me, dollface," he commanded.

And his gravelly voice, coupled with his fullness everywhere, spilled me over the edge.

I came in waves, convulsing around him.

"Fuck!" He hissed, finding his release.

His head rested on the middle of my back, his breath warm on my spine. After a beat, he rolled off me, discarding his hot liquid.

I lay on his bed, royally fucked and pissed off I'd be missing this all of my life. "Is it always this good with you?"

He smirked. "What, your exes never fucked you like that?"

"I've only had three partners, and no, not even close," I said truthfully. They were more interested in getting themselves off. Nothing with any of the three partners I had was even remotely this hot.

He shot up his brow. "Three?"

"I won't even ask how many you've had. Your reputation speaks for itself."

I picked an imaginary piece of lint off the sheet, then gazed back up.

He raked his fingers through his dark hair. "Over three, dollface."

"I think we're both going straight to hell," I said, echoing his earlier words.

"I definitely am," he said, and his grin disappeared.

There was that side of him again. Mysterious, like he was holding out on me.

"I have to take a shower."

"Should we talk about this?"

"No, I'm already late." He stalked toward his marble shower.

"Can I shower with you?"

He turned, and I twisted my lips into a smile.

"I think we know how that's going to end, and I'm already late."

"I'll make it worth your while."

He laughed. "Maybe you aren't so innocent after all, but no. And for the record, I don't do sleepovers."

He shut the door behind him, and I flopped back on his bed, pulled the pillow over my head, and screamed into it.

* * *

He left without saying goodbye. I was in the shower but left my door open. He could've come in.

Even though I'd scrubbed the smell of sex off me, his manly Barrett scent remained. Or maybe it was etched in my mind, I couldn't be sure. I felt sore but in a good way. A satisfied way.

The last twenty-four hours replayed in my mind. Barrett found me at the hotel and berated me for my scandalous outfit. But judging by his subtle glaring gazes on my body at the party he later accompanied me to, he liked scandalous things.

When I sat on his lap, I had already consumed a few glasses of champagne. It gave me the courage to intentionally rub against his groin, ever so slightly—just enough for him to swell beneath me.

Grace whispered something in my ear before he took me home. Three words that excited me. "Go get him." The idea was fleeting when everything faded to black. That was until four o'clock in the morning when I woke up. Knowing he stripped me out of my dress sent goosebumps up my arms. That could easily weird one out, but it didn't. I wanted Barrett to want me like I wanted him. I wanted to give him pleasure as he'd shown me.

His heated glances and rough touches hours earlier were all I thought about when I climbed back into bed after scrubbing my face clean. So what was a girl meant to do?

If you asked my mother—which you absolutely shouldn't—she'd have said to stay clear. Wait for the next charity event or dinner party when she'd have a perfect suitor lined up for me. But what did I do? Exactly the opposite of what they expected of a Diamond heir. I marched straight into his room, stripped naked for him, and practically begged him to fuck me.

* * *

"Wakey-wakey." Grace's voice rang in my ear, bringing me back to the sound of the crashing waves and the searing sun.

I groaned and pushed the sun hat off my face. "How long have I been asleep?" Too long. My neck and stomach burned. I sat upright and glanced down at my torso. Red and sunburned. My string bikini offered zero protection from the hot afternoon sun.

"Oh, shit." Grace regarded me.

"You think? I look like the main course at the Lobster Inn."

"You, of all people, need sunscreen with your white skin."

"Yes, thank you, Grace. But I'm afraid I'm two hours too late for that!"

"There you are!" Pepper approached us.

"Lourde, oh my God, what did you do?"

I groaned. Her eyes trailed from my face to my stomach. "If you want a tan, you should know with your skin color, you only get two choices… albino or devil red. Bronze isn't an option."

"Hilarious. Do you think I was trying to go for this?"

I stood up. Ouch. Just folding to stand, and my skin hurt. I had to get some aloe vera from the pharmacy, *stat.*

"Wait. What happened last night with Barrett?"

"I've been asking her all morning," Grace said.

"Well, I thought I'd wait till you both here, but now I'm seriously burned. I'll have to make it quick."

"Finally!" Grace sighed in frustration.

"Okay, so I may have seduced him."

"Oh, hell yes," Pepper said, flopping on my sun chair. "And?"

"And…" I thought about how he'd manhandled me—his fingers inside both holes. The way his lips roughly left their bruising mark on my neck. Mind-blowing orgasms…

"Lourde Diamond, are you blushing?" Grace asked.

"Holy hell. I think he's ruined sex for me for all eternity."

Pepper let out a yelp before adding, "Well, you've only had a handful of boyfriends."

"Trust me. If I'd slept with a thousand men, it wouldn't matter. Him and me together, I don't know, it's just…" I fanned myself with my free hand. "I'm all hot just thinking about it."

Grace and Pepper exchanged glances. "Anyway, I don't need to tell you this, girls, but we lock this down. No one, and I mean, *no one*, is to find out, especially Dane and Jake. I'm sure it's only a one-off anyway… okay twice." I slid my hair behind my ear and split into a grin. He was quick to turn me down but just as quick to want me and fuck me. Maybe we could continue doing whatever it was we were doing.

"Uh-huh," Pepper said.

"Once or twice? Hell no, Lourde. Why stop?" Grace asked.

"Yeah, why stop?" Pepper asked in agreement.

"We'll see. Anyway, he might just reject me again. He likes to do that. I would. He'd be fucking a lobster, and I don't know about you two, but I wouldn't fuck me looking like this." I dragged my hand down my sunburned body.

They both laughed.

"I don't know. I saw how he looked at you last night at the party when he thought no one was watching. I spotted the lust in his eyes," Pepper added. A tingle of warmth slashed across my chest, knowing he was watching me from afar. But what else did I want from him?

"Lourde, I know what you're thinking, and don't go there. Barrett isn't the relationship type." Pepper crossed her arms over her chest.

"Oh no, I know that." I picked up my beach bag, losing the ridiculous thought that Barrett could ever want more from me.

"Not to mention the Connor factor," Grace added.

"Ah yes, there's that too." I'd hate to think what my brother would do if he found out. But there was no way he would. I wasn't telling him, and neither was Barrett. And I trusted my girls. They wouldn't tell a soul. "I need to rectify this situation," I said, peering down my inflamed body.

"Yes, you do," Grace agreed, and Pepper knowingly nodded.

"If this miraculously improves, I'll text you later."

"Get some lotion and sit out of the sun for a few days."

"It's Friday!" I groaned.

"There'll be more parties," Grace stated. Plus, I think Dane wanted a movie night, which was code for *sex session.*

"You know I never had that. With any of my exes, I mean. Sex was just average. But I didn't know any different. I have a new benchmark now, and I love it. I'm screwed, though, because no one will ever be as good as Barrett between the sheets."

"Well, Jake can't get me off as well as my vibrator. And Mr. Vee expects nothing in return. If I could marry him, I would." Pepper deadpanned.

I laughed. "Ow, that hurt my stomach muscles."

"Go!" Pepper said.

"Okay, I'm going. Love you, girls," I said, waving goodbye and trudging off through the hot sand.

I felt my phone vibrate in my striped beach bag. Pulling it out, the word 'Mother' flashed on the screen. Damn. I hadn't called her back after she left a few messages since arriving in the Hamptons.

"Hi, Momma."

"Lourde, darling. How are the Hamptons?"

"Lovely, Mom. How's everything at the house?"

"Your brother tells me you moved in with Barrett?"

Of course, that's her lead-in. "Yes, I did, after I caught Hunter cheating on me."

"Yes, yes. That wasn't ideal. But how lovely of Barrett to take you in."

"Ideal? No Mother, it most certainly wasn't ideal."

"Well, forget about Hunter. The good news is I have found someone perfect for you."

"Like Hunter that you thought was perfect?"

"Hush, darling. Onward and upward. I'd like you to come home next Friday night where we can have dinner with the whole family. Your brother will be there, and so will Finigan Connolly. You see, Finigan's father, James, is an acquaintance of your father's, and he is popping by before he and his wife jet off to Cannes for the summer. His son is staying in Manhattan, so it's the perfect opportunity for both families to meet."

"Mom, please. I think I might take a break from dating. I just want to be single for a while."

"Nonsense. You aren't getting any younger, you know."

"I'm twenty-three!"

"Well, I was married to your father at twenty-one, so you're already behind, and time is ticking away. You know, with privilege comes responsibility. Finigan's father is the Governor of Massachusetts. The family is old money with a long line of respectable politicians going back to the early 1900s."

Wow. So what?

"Come home, darling. If only for the evening. Then

you can pop back to the Hamptons and be with Pepper and Grace. Take the helicopter this time if you want to."

I knew she only wanted the best for me, but honestly, meeting Finigan was the last thing I wanted. Worse, I knew if I didn't come back, she'd hound me every day until I did. "Okay, Mom."

"Marvelous. I'll ask the chefs to prepare your favorite."

"Great," I drawled, hoping she couldn't hear me rolling my eyes.

I hung up, determined more than ever to make the limited time I had with Barrett count.

17

BARRETT

I heard groans coming from her room. I leaped the steps two by two, hastily walking to her ajar door.

When I'd pushed it the rest of the way open, I wasn't sure what I'd expected, but it certainly wasn't a lobster clam bake. Lourde was naked with a red chest and stomach with white triangular patches over her tits where her bikini once was.

"Jesus, fuck, are you trying to get melanoma?"

"I heard you coming. Thought what's the point of covering up. And no, I'm not trying to get melanoma. I fell asleep on the sand. I didn't get too much sleep last night, remember?" A slow grin spread across her face.

I was annoyed with her, but it didn't stop me from entering or kneeling in front of her, assessing the damage on her skin.

"Ever heard of sunscreen? Usually, you apply before you fall asleep."

"Pepper and Grace have already given me the third degree."

"You're lucky these aren't third-degree burns!" I ran

my hand down the middle of her chest. Her skin was scorching hot and would only get worse if not treated.

I looked down at the bottle next to her and picked it up, scanning its contents.

"This is shit. You need a burn cream."

"And you know this, Dr. Black, with the Ph.D. you have hidden in your sock drawer?"

She put her hands back on the bed, leaning back, so her breasts pointed toward me. Sunburned to a crisp, and my dick still bulged in my pants. Distraction was necessary. I dug my phone out and scrolled to find Calvin, my on-call doctor.

"Calvin, it's Barrett. Can you come to the house and bring some burn cream, the one that's got the hydrogel?"

"Of course. Are you okay?"

"Yes, fine. Grab an antibiotic ointment too." I scanned her, and she stared at me, wide-eyed.

Her face wasn't burned. She must have slept with a hat on. At least that was something.

"Sure. See you in fifteen minutes."

I slid the phone back into my pocket.

"How do you know so much about burns?"

"Evelyn got burned badly when we were kids." Okay, that slipped out. I'd never shared that with anyone, yet it rolled off the tongue. Being naked, she distracted me. Obviously.

"I'm sorry. That must have been awful for you all. I've never heard you really speak about Evelyn before."

Awful was right. If you call my father intentionally pouring a cup of scorching tea on her head awful, you'd be damn right.

"Yeah, well, she lives in Boston. I don't see her much."

"That's a shame. I think families are everything."

She is my only family.

She regarded me, and it was enough about my family. It was already too much. "You seem to have an interesting relationship with your mother."

"Yeah." She puffed out her cheeks in a long exhalation. "I love her to bits, but she doesn't understand me."

She grabbed her floral dress beside her and slipped it over her head. I zeroed in on her tits before the dress covered them.

"Oh, shit!"

She was stuck, wasn't she? Goddamn, even the sides of her arms were red as they extended over her head.

"Jesus, Lourde, can't you do anything?" I leaned over and gently tugged her arm through the arm strap.

"Sorry!" She scowled. "If I'm an inconvenience, just leave. You're the one who barged in here."

I blew out my cheeks. Vulnerable Lourde wasn't something I was used to.

"I know you've probably never cared for anyone your whole life, so I'm not asking you to start now. I can figure it out—"

"That's not true." I sat beside her. "I've had to care for Evelyn."

She pulled the floral dress down, covering her creamy thighs. "When she was burned?"

"Yes."

She held my gaze. "And when my parents died."

"How old were you when they passed?"

Passed. That was such a delicate word. How about, how old were you when you held the gun that killed your mother, and your father shot himself in the head straight after?

"Sixteen and Evelyn was eighteen."

"Oh, Barrett, I couldn't imagine what that time must have been like for you."

I didn't bother to respond. I wasn't looking for pity.

"Wait, why wasn't she the one taking care of you? She was eighteen. You were sixteen."

Oh, fuck, how to get out of this one? "She had injuries." I looked up at Lourde. She was looking at me, wanting more, but I couldn't give her any more.

"And I'm guessing you didn't."

"No," I said quietly, the image haunting me.

"I see." She cleared her throat. "Well, thank you for calling the doctor."

"It's nothing," I said, getting up from beside her. "I'll send him up when he arrives."

"That's okay. I'll wait for him in the living room."

I glanced over my shoulder, and she lifted her stare. In all that pain, and her eyes still drifted to my ass? I walked out and grinned.

Leaving Lourde with the good doctor for fifteen minutes was enough time. I left the study and walked back into the living room, where the doctor had his hand on her stomach. Pain from clenching my teeth radiated up my jaw.

"Barrett." Lourde took me in, her focus now on me rather than Calvin.

"How are we going in here, Doc?"

Calvin removed his hand from Lourde's skin when he saw me. "Ms. Diamond should recover fine. If she applies this ointment twice a day, religiously for the next two weeks, there shouldn't be any permanent damage to the skin."

"Thank you so much for coming," she said, placing her hand on the doctor's hand.

"Pleasure, Ms. Diamond," he said, staring at her in a way that definitely crossed the fucking line.

The good-looking young doctor ought to fuck off, and

what the fuck was she doing sending him a signal only a guy would interpret as something more than friendly.

"Right. Lourde probably should rest. Thanks for coming out. I'm sure you have a load of coked-up freshmen to attend to."

Lourde scowled at me, and I narrowed my eyes. The doctor quickly packed up his medicine bag and kept pace as I walked him out.

"This is for you. Thanks again." I handed him an envelope with a generous check and shut the front door.

"Goodby—"

I walked back into the living room, where she sat on the lounge reading the bottle of ointment, and I took a seat in my armchair facing the ocean. "So?"

"So?" she echoed.

"You wanted to talk to me this morning."

She sat upright and put the bottle down. This ought to be interesting.

"Well, I… okay…" She paused.

Was she nervous?

She steadied her gaze. "I want more of this," she said without a shred of hesitation.

"I told you, I don't do relationships."

"I don't want a relationship."

That's a first. Usually, I couldn't get women to leave me alone.

"I'm here till Friday. Then I'm not sure if I'm coming back or staying in Manhattan."

My stomach did something fucking weird. *Haven't I eaten?*

"I thought you were here for the summer?"

"Lucky for you, I have to go back to Manhattan. My mother rang. She is planning a dinner and wants me to be there. She's promised the man she has is perfect for me. Says he'll be the one." She cocked an eyebrow.

"The one? Is that right? If you don't want a relationship, what do you want?"

She picked up the bottle of ointment. "Someone to rub the lotion on me."

I laughed.

She set the bottle down again, and her eyes heated. "And someone to fuck for the next seven days before I have to settle down again."

My dick came to life. "I like it when you talk dirty, dollface."

"But we have one problem with your…" I circled my fingers. "Ruse, shall we call it?"

"What?" she questioned with a whisper.

"Brother boy."

"Well, if he finds out, it won't be good."

"No, it definitely won't."

"My lips are sealed."

I uncrossed my legs and moved opposite her, unscrewing the lotion bottle. Before I peeled down a strap, I squeezed the ointment on my hand and slid my hand over her scorching hot skin.

"Does that mean we have a deal?" Our gazes collided, and I dipped my hand lower, massaging her breast. Momentarily, she closed her eyes, and my skin heated, knowing how much I turned her on.

"Seven days, dollface. My cock, your pussy for one week. Then it's like it never happened."

"It's like it never happened." She nodded slowly, and my hand dragged down to her thighs. I lifted the dress over her head carefully, then kneeled in front of her, spreading her legs.

"Kiss me, Barrett."

I glanced up. *Did she want my lips on hers again?* No, way too intimate.

She pushed my shoulders down. That fucking minx.

The truth was, I'd been thinking about eating her out all day.

"Spread your legs," I ordered and pushed her thighs aside. She wasn't wearing underwear.

Fuck, I just got harder. "You're very naughty."

"Only for you," she sighed.

She wanted this as much as I did.

I darted my tongue between her. She was already wet and ready for me. I groaned. Lourde tasted so sweet. The sweetest of them all, and I wanted to please her. Be the one fuck she'd never forget, etched in her mind like a goddamn tattoo. The thought of her with this other guy made me angrier as I fucked her with my tongue feverishly.

"Ah, Barrett, fuck." She arched her back, her knees around my head.

I pushed her knees to the side, knowing she'd feel me more deeply that way. I dared to look up. She opened her eyes and stared down at me. "What are you doing? Don't stop!" Her cheeks glowed pink, lips red and ever so fuckable. I was so hot for her, it was ridiculous.

I grinned.

"You're an ass," she said and grabbed my hair with all her might.

My dick throbbed harder as I plunged back in, fucking her in and out, deeper and alternating between her fuckhole and her clit until her legs quivered and pussy spasmed. Her breath was ragged, and her body tensed. "Fuck, Barrett," she screamed and pulsed around my tongue. I licked up every drop of her. She lay back on the lounge, and impatiently, I thumbed my pants down. I'd already wrapped myself by the time she opened her eyes. I climbed on top of her. Missionary, fuck it, I didn't care. I couldn't wait any longer to claim her.

She pulled me into her chest, and my tip found her entrance. "Fuck me." I bared my teeth as I sunk into her. I entered her, pushing deeper, feeling her warm, wet, delicious cunt. "I could fuck you all day long, dollface," I groaned.

Her hands were on my face, pulling me down to hers. She melted her lips to mine. Her tongue found me as we feverishly tangled. *And I could kiss you too.*

I pulled away first and found her staring at me.

"Fuck me harder," she whispered, and I forgot about the feeling of her lips on mine a second ago and did what I did best. Fuck.

Lourde's hands gripped my ass, squeezing me into her. Heat gripped my body as my muscles tensed.

"Ah," she yelled through her labored breath, finding her release.

I closed my eyes, and a heat slashed my chest. And when I felt her hand on my cheek, I opened my eyes to find her staring into my soul. A deep throaty sound escaped my mouth as I found my release staring into her hazelly-greens.

18

LOURDE

"So, I asked him to be my fuck buddy."

The waiter set our glasses down at precisely the wrong moment, and we all burst into laughter. He glanced at me, then retreated.

"Hopefully, he didn't recognize me!"

"Girl, you're in the society pages. Of course, he did," Grace said.

"Screw him. He's just jealous it's not him," Pepper said, scraping the last of her lunch.

"I can't believe you asked Barrett. You know he's had more women than your brother," Pepper added.

"Ew." I really don't want to put my brother's name in this equation. "And I don't care. We're just using each other for the time being."

"And how long is that?" Grace asked, taking a sip of her lemon-infused water. "Surely, he has to get back to controlling his own company in Manhattan soon? I'm surprised he's been here for this long."

"He's working on a deal here."

"And you have nothing to do with why he's been here this long?" Pepper's eyebrows shot into her forehead.

"Doubtful." Although a tiny part of me hoped if I came back, he'd still be here.

I picked at the rest of my lobster salad.

"I have to go back on Friday. Mom's hosting a dinner with Governor Connolly of Massachusetts, his wife, and his son."

"Finigan Connolly?" Grace questioned.

"Yes."

"He's cute."

"Great," I said automatically and not at all interested. I couldn't get Barrett out of my mind. All I could think about was what we were going to do tonight.

"Wow, that enthusiasm is next level," Grace mocked, but I didn't care.

"She's thinking about Barrett's throbbing member." Pepper smirked, and I laughed.

"Told you!" Pepper laughed.

"Well, I think if you only have a week, make it a week Barrett will never forget. I know a lingerie place…" She stood up and flung her Yves Saint Laurent quilted tote over her shoulder.

"What?"

"Yeah, come on, it will be fun. It's a new store in East Hampton, hidden and exclusive. Right up your alley. I walked past yesterday. It's new. A designer out of LA. She loves everything lace, straps, and gold only."

I threw back the rest of my champagne. My toes tingled. The idea of dressing sexy for Barrett was intriguing and exhilarating. "Let's do it."

We walked the cobblestone pathways, the afternoon sun beating down and casting shadows. My skin still hurt, but the cream he massaged into me last night and this morning was definitely helping. Or maybe it was the blistering touch of his hand that made me forget the pain of the sunburn.

One thing I hadn't forgotten was the pain in his eyes when he spoke about his sister, Evelyn, being burned. It was then that he spoke of his parents, and I wondered what he was leaving out of the story to make him feel so much pain.

"Here it is!" Pepper shrieked.

I stopped and turned. The storefront wasn't bright and open like the others, rather the opposite. Dark and with a small entrance, I realized we were in an alley. "What's this?"

"I told you, she's new. Her stuff is rude, not for your regular Hamptonite… hence, the Fort Knox entrance."

"I'm definitely intrigued now."

Pepper rang the bell, and a woman wearing a see-through top, lace bra, and short skirt with suspenders opened the door. Oh my, she looked phenomenal. "Okay, now I see why there's a closed door and no display," I whispered to Grace.

"Ladies, do come in."

"We haven't got an appointment," Grace said.

"That's all right. We can accommodate you. Ms. Diamond, pleasure to meet you. I'm Daisy. Part owner of Rose Lace. Do come in."

"Thanks."

The store was gorgeous, simple, and had three racks, two on either side with garments on each, then the back rack, which had bridal corsets. Lace meets BDSM was the style, and I loved it.

"Oh, my." I thought about wearing everything in here and parading it in front of Barrett. I wanted to drive him nuts like he had driven me. This was exactly what I needed.

"This is gorgeous." I picked up a lace bra, tasteful but skirting on the border of dirty. It was emerald green and so fragile.

"This one just came in." She picked it off the hanger. "We like to pair it with this." She held up a thong with a belt.

"My boyfriend is going to love this," Pepper said, picking up something on the other rack.

"That's the idea. My wife loves these," she said, picking up the purple halter bra with satin cups. Oh, I loved it too. In fact, I loved everything in here as I looked around.

"Go try it all on. Let me open a bottle of champagne for you girls. I'll be right back."

"Thank you!" Like a kid in a candy shop, I was excited and overwhelmed, but this felt so much more than that.

I was famished from trying on lingerie and spending the entire afternoon laughing and parading the gorgeous pieces with Pepper, Grace, and the store owner, Daisy.

All that shopping had burned off the small salad I'd had for lunch. I raided Barrett's refrigerator when I got home and spotted two steaks. His housekeeper must have restocked it this morning. Perfect. In fact, I whipped out my phone.

Lourde: *What time will you be back? I'm making dinner.*

Before I could put my phone back on the bench, it beeped.

Barrett: *Ten minutes. I'm hungry.*

Lourde: *Good*

Barrett: *Not for food.*

My stomach flipped, and a grin spread into my cheeks.

Lourde: *A man's got to eat.*
Barrett: *Oh, I'll eat.*

Exhilaration shot up my spine. Anticipation for our evening ahead was too much. Quickly, I ran upstairs and changed into my favorite lingerie piece, the emerald green set, and threw my sundress over it. He wouldn't know what hit him.

As I walked down the stairs, I heard the front door click open, followed by footsteps. When I reached the final step, there he stood in his crisp white shirt and navy suit that molded to his broad shoulders.

"Hey, handsome," I said, staring into his dark eyes. At this level, we were the same height.

I pecked him on the cheek, and he glared at me with a perplexed look on his face. "Is this what husbands and wives do?" he asked.

I shrugged. "I wouldn't know." The thought of greeting Barrett every day sent a blush up my neck.

"I'm getting changed." He side-eyed me then disappeared, taking the stairs two at a time.

Okay, maybe I shouldn't have done that. I didn't know what came over me. I just leaned up to kiss him. He looked handsome, arrogant, and strong in his suit. His scent of wood and leather was too nice to pass up.

I seared the steak in the hot griddle pan, making the crisscross lines on it, and paired it with blanched beans and almond flakes drizzled with butter. Even *my* mouth was watering.

Walking down in casual sweatpants, he pulled over a white shirt, his muscle pack flexed and moved with the motion.

"Let's eat," he said, staring at me.

Fuck the food. I couldn't care less now.

But he sat down, which was a cue for me to get the plates and forget about his blinding muscles until later.

"Smells good, Lourde."

"Steak, rare, with green beans."

"I can see that." He grinned, slicing into it.

It was perfectly cooked, too, by the color of pink on his slice.

"I didn't know you cooked."

"We have chefs, but I like to join them in the kitchen sometimes."

"Why?" And what do Mommy and Daddy think about consorting with the help?"

"They don't know."

"Ah-ha."

"Well, Mom caught me there once. The pastry chef, Tatiana, was teaching me how to roll out and make croissants, which is a serious art, by the way. Since then, I usually sneak in when Mom's out shopping or with her friends."

"Well, cook for me anytime. I mostly eat out."

"Alone?"

"Sometimes. Sometimes for dinner meetings like the other night in the hotel."

"Doesn't it get lonely?"

"No." He shrugged. "I like it alone."

"I see. So, how was your day anyway?"

"*Now,* you sound like a wife."

I laughed, and the corners of his mouth peeled into a smile. "Long."

"Any closer to completing that hotel deal?"

"Soon now."

"Oh?" I put down my cutlery. "So that means you'll go back too?"

He looked at me, heat pooling behind his eyes. "I'm the boss, Lourde. I can do what I want."

Why did I feel we weren't talking about work anymore?

"And what is it you want?" I lowered my voice to a whisper.

"Right now? Dessert." He pushed his plate to the side.

I twisted my lips into a grin. I stood up and slowly pulled down my sundress. It fell to my ankles, and I stepped out of it. I stood there in nothing but my new lingerie with one hand on my hip. "This kind of dessert?"

"Fuck me, Lourde." He stared. His gaze slowly tracked me from head to toe, then he wiped his mouth with the napkin.

"Turn around," he commanded, and his voice sent me weak at the knees. I did as he asked, turning around slowly, my bare ass clothed in a tiny lace thong. A groan fell from his mouth, and it reverberated between my legs.

I glanced over my shoulder. "Follow me."

"No."

I whipped my head around, but he was already behind me, lifting me in his arms.

"What are you doing?" I shrieked.

"I can't wait that long." He took the stairs two at a time with me in his arms. I gripped his broad shoulders as he carried me with ease, then threw me on his bed, admiring me. I climbed back over to the side of the bed where he stood and looked up at him. I clawed his sweatpants down, eager to taste him with my mouth.

"What do you think you're doing?"

"Having *my* dessert."

Without waiting for him to reply, I freed his erection, and it sprung free, thick and hard.

Knowing I did this to him was too much to take. I

wrapped my lips around his delicious head, teasingly, swiping it with my tongue.

"Ah." He titled his head back as his hands circled my hair.

I went up and down, deeper and deeper, taking him all. I didn't care if I gagged. He was huge, and I wanted him. I needed to show him I wasn't this little innocent Diamond heir. I was dirty and only for him. He guided me with his hand. Gently, then firmly.

"Fuck me, dollface. You give magnificent head."

I squeezed his balls, then swiped them once over with my tongue. He groaned a throaty groan, and the sound had me dripping with arousal. As if reading my thoughts, he trailed a finger down my back, finding my wet spot. I moaned along his girth.

"Stop, I'll come," he said, pushing me away and wrapping his hand around my jaw.

I looked up. "Good, I want you to."

Ignoring his drunk eyes, I wrapped my mouth around his tip, then to the base, repeating the motion until I felt him tremble beneath me.

"Fuck!" He roared, gripping my hair between his hands. Hot liquid shot down my throat, and I swallowed all of him, making sure I didn't miss a drop. I used the back of my hand to wipe my mouth while staring up at him.

He stood, his eyes wide.

Who said I was innocent?

* * *

After giving me two mind-blowing orgasms, I lay exhausted and satisfied. The man knew every move in the Kama Sutra. But I wasn't complaining, far from it. With my boyfriends, the sex went from okay to average. With Barrett, it just kept getting better.

"So I have to go out on the boat tomorrow for a client's boring lunch thing. If you're not doing anything with the girls, do you want to come?" He turned to me.

"I'd love to," I said, surprised by his question.

"Don't get any ideas. It's just… the guys are all bringing their partners so… you know." He sat up in bed, and I did the same.

"What ideas might I be getting? I know we're fuck buddies, Barrett, that's all."

He nodded. Then why did part of me feel like maybe this was a date?

I climbed out of his bed, left my lingerie in his room, and walked out naked.

"Night," I said, shutting the door behind me.

19

BARRETT

"**N**o, Dad, stop," I screamed.

"Barrett, let go, you stupid child."

I wrangled the gun, holding it tight so he couldn't pry it from my hands, but he was bigger and stronger than me. He rolled on top of me. I extended my arms so they were over my head, but his grip was too strong. He punched me in the side, and the sickening crack sounded, followed by excruciating pain. I took one hand off the gun, curling my hands around my rib cage, trying to protect it from further blows.

"Let him go, Jason," Mom screamed.

Bang.

My sister screamed. She held her thigh, looking at her bloodied hand.

"Evelyn," I yelled.

"Eve!" Mom raced toward her. My grip around the gun loosened as I paled.

"This is all your fault, Violet." He spat, his weight crushing my bruised ribs. Then, before I knew what was happening, his fingers curled around the trigger, and he pressed it once, pointing it directly in front of me at Mom.

Bang.

I screamed. The bullet pierced her chest. Her eyes widened, then she fell.

"Mom! No!"

I rolled away from him and scrambled toward her as Evelyn screamed, and he yelled. But all I could see was the blood pooling underneath her. Her face paled, and a tear fell down her cheek.

"Mom, stay with me." I pressed down on her chest.

"Stay strong, baby boy," she whispered in a shallow breath. Then closed her eyes.

"Mom!" I frantically screamed.

"Now, look what you did, Barrett." He got up off his knees and pointed the gun at me.

With my bloodied hands on Mom, I held my breath, shaking.

"Dad, please!" Evelyn cried out, backed against a wall. Her leg poured out blood.

He turned to my sister.

No. You weren't taking her too. With a blinding rage, I got up and started running toward him.

He gave me a wry smile, then turned the gun on himself.

Bang.

"Barrett!"

I felt a warmth on my cheek.

"Wake up, Barrett."

My heart was beating erratically, my chest rising and falling quickly. Sweat bubbled on my brow. I blinked a few times, adjusting before opening my eyes. Lourde's shadowy face was strained, her brows knitted together as she kneeled over me.

Fuck, a nightmare. I hadn't had one in some time, but it was always the same nightmare on repeat.

"Are you okay?" She put her hand on my heart. "Jesus, Barrett, your heart is racing."

"I'm okay." I couldn't tell her I had a nightmare, could I?

"I heard you yell out in your sleep. I think you were having a nightmare."

I blinked. "Yeah, I think so."

"Shh, it's okay." Her soothing hand stroked my cheek, and the feeling calmed me down.

"I'm okay," I repeated, slowing my breathing.

"Good. I'll let you sleep now." She lowered her hand from my face, but I reached out for her arm.

"You can stay." She stilled. "Only if you want."

Silently, she slid under the sheets beside me. I wrapped my arms around her, and she pressed her back into my chest. Warmth and calm washed over me. Then I drifted off to sleep.

* * *

Okay, I'll admit it was weird as fuck waking up with a woman in my bed, but it wasn't just any woman. It was my best friend, Connor's sister. What was weirder was I agreed to her little fuck-buddy pact.

With her still in my bed asleep, I inched out. I left instructions downstairs on the kitchen counter about where we were meeting today and noticed that my housekeeper had restocked the fridge full of Lourde's favorite yogurt. Now, I liked it too. *So what?* I was just being polite, asking her to buy more.

My morning dragged with mundane Zoom calls and a meeting in East Hampton until it didn't anymore, and it was time to get the fuck out and see her.

The sun beat down on the wooden marina, the ninety-foot royal blue power yacht moored at the pier. I walked across the wood planks toward her. She hadn't noticed me yet, but I had her. Like a walking, talking felony, she stood at the marina waiting for me. Wearing a long yellow dress that lifted in the breeze and a tan belt that cinched in tight at her waist, her naturally wavy hair swept across her shoulders, and I had to remember to breathe.

I shouldered out of my jacket, flinging it over my arm. When I looked up again, she was staring at me. Her smile reached her hazel eyes and made me feel warm all over.

What the fuck, Barrett?

First, I invited her to sleep in my bed, then this? I couldn't wait for the next five days to be up. Then my head could be out of the goddamn Lourde clouds.

"Hello, dollface," I whispered, so the men behind me couldn't hear.

"Hello, handsome." She kissed me on the cheek, aware of glaring eyes. "Is this how husbands and wives would greet each other?" she asked.

"I'd tongue your pussy if it were only us, but as you can see, we have company."

She laughed, then threw a hand over her mouth. "My, oh, my."

"Lourde Diamond, I thought that was you." She lowered her hand and straightened, her composure returning.

"Lourde, this is a colleague of mine, Fred Basset, and next to him, we have Caleb Johnson."

"Lovely to meet you, Lourde."

"Lourde is a dear friend," I said, instantly dispelling any rumors.

She held my gaze for a moment, then turned, smiling at both men. "Lovely to meet you both."

"Fred and Caleb were the architects on 21 Park."

"The lines are stunning on that building, groundbreaking. I hope you charged my dear *friend* here a bucketload for that award-winning design."

Laughter surrounded me, and I couldn't help but smirk. I didn't miss the emphasis she placed on the word 'friend.' *Touché.* I wrapped my hand around her waist, directing her onboard, and subtly, I squeezed her. "Shall we?"

"Oh, absolutely." She grinned, tossing her hair over her shoulder.

* * *

I peered over. Lourde talked animatedly with the wives of the men on board. She held the audience of the women even if she didn't even know it.

"Lourde Diamond is a special friend to have. Would you agree, Barrett?"

Of course, Fred would pry. The guy was a weasel but the best architect on the East Coast.

"Actually, it's the friendship of her brother I value."

"He's taking over from his father soon if the rumors are true," Fred added.

"Are rumors ever true, Fred?"

"Sometimes…"

Okay, that's enough.

"Maybe when they discuss your mistress in Sweden?"

He opened his mouth to speak, then shut it. His eyes darted to the left, where his wife was chatting with a group of women. I knew she wasn't in earshot.

"How could you possibly know that?"

"My business is to know everything about the people I'm in business with."

"Right, well." He threw his whiskey back, narrowed his eyes, then walked away.

"Bye, Fred," I said.

I walked over to Lourde and overheard talking about the editor of one of her family's magazines. "What he should do is write less propaganda and more about the facts. But don't tell my brother that!" They all laughed, then she spotted me and turned around.

"Ladies," I said.

"Barrett." Fred's wife smiled and pushed her newly fake tits up, straightening her back.

"So lovely to see you all here in the Hamptons, but I'm afraid I have to pull Ms. Diamond away from you all now as we have dinner plans."

"Oh, lovely. Have fun, you two." She gave me a pointed grin.

"Not sure we will. It's with a client," I said, getting the queen bees of the society pages off the gossip trail.

"Oh, no fun!" Caleb's wife laughed wickedly.

"A woman's duty, isn't that right, Lourde?" The wife said, rolling her eyes. "I can't tell you how many boring dinners I've been to."

"I'm suddenly feeling ill," Lourde said, fanning herself.

Quickly, I scanned her. *What was wrong?* Her mouth edged into a sly grin.

I laughed. "Sure you are."

"So nice to meet you all." She turned to her new friends and kissed their cheeks before waving goodbye. I watched the women as they wished they had the same natural and flawless body she did.

We were walking along the marina when she turned to me. "So dinner, huh?" she questioned, gripping my elbow as she nearly tripped on the hardwood plank.

"I had to get off that boat."

"Ah, I see." We walked in silence for a few more minutes.

"Are you hungry?" I asked.

"Famished. There were only little canapes on the boat, and if I have any more champagne, I'll float away."

"Well, we don't want that now. Who'll give me splendid head if you're not here?"

"Barrett! Shh!"

I didn't give a fuck. The strangers that walked past us were just that, strangers. Plus, if it meant I got to see the faint dusting of blush creep on her cheeks, I'd shout it from the rooftops.

20

LOURDE

I thought he was on a business call when he walked ahead of me, but he'd arranged a picnic by the beach and all in less than an hour.

My dress floated around my ankles in the afternoon breeze. Barrett walked beside me as we leisurely strolled the piers, where people gathered for pre-dinner drinks and nibbles. Soft music filled the space, and waves gently crashed against the weathered pylons.

I glanced at Barrett. Sunlight caught his eyes as he tossed me a carefree smile. A warmth slashed my chest as a calm came over me. A calm I didn't have at home. The idea of going back filled me with anxiety. With a spacious duplex penthouse, how could I feel stifled by Mom and Dad? Maybe it was time I moved out. Have this dinner with Finigan and then look for somewhere else to live.

He passed through the throngs of people, and I realized I'd fallen behind. "Come on, keep up." He turned and slowed his pace. "I don't want to lose you to the hungry eyes out there."

"You should talk," I said, noticing hungry women ogle

him as we passed the last of the tables. That perfect head he was talking about? Any woman here would line up around the block for Barrett Black. He looked around as if he didn't realize they were staring at him. His face blanched as his brows pinched lower.

Did he not want the attention?

* * *

He'd set it all up—a blanket, picnic basket, containers filled with fresh seafood and salads, and two beers. We sat hidden in an alcove of reeds and dunes on a secluded section of the beach. The ocean was like a sheet of glass in front of us.

"Thought you might like the taste of a proper drink." He smiled, handing me the icy bottle.

"I've had beer before."

He tilted his perfect face. "I doubt that."

"Okay, maybe that's not entirely true. Mom would die a thousand deaths if she knew I was about to drink from a bottle."

I tried unscrewing the lid but only pinched my skin.

I watched him slam down the bottle against the edge of the basket. The lid popped off, and he held it out for me.

Not one to be outplayed, I did the same. *Dammit.* The lid didn't budge.

He laughed. "Let me show you."

He put his hand on top of mine, and a weird feeling settled at the base of my spine.

"Ready?" he asked. "One, two, three." Together, we yanked the top of the lid. The froth bubbled and spilled over. Quickly, I took my lips to the bottle's edge, swallowing the frothy liquid.

"Now there's an image." He grinned.

The crisp malt flavor was delicious. "This is good," I said, eventually.

"Don't get used to it, dollface. Diamond women don't drink beer."

I groaned. "Diamond women also don't consort with mysterious men."

"Mysterious?" He chuckled. Putting the beer to his lips, he took a large sip. I watched his Adam's apple bob up and down, and heat coursed through me.

"And are you satisfied?" he questioned.

I blushed. "Yes, very."

"I'm not talking about us, Lourde." He laughed. "I don't need to ask if you're satisfied. I hear it when you scream my name."

I rolled my lips in on themselves. Damn, his dirty words were like poetry to my lady parts.

"Are you satisfied?" I asked, scraping my teeth across my bottom lip.

He lowered his eyes. My chest heated, and I stopped trying to open the food container.

Shit. How can he still level me with one look?

"Did you not hear me when I said you give the best head I've ever had?"

I shook my head. "But you've had every available woman in Manhattan."

He laughed. And a piece inside me slowly died. He hadn't denied it.

"How 'bout the best cunt I've ever tasted." His flinty gaze leveled me, speechless. He took a swig of his beer. "Besides, you didn't answer my question."

What question? My thoughts were fuzzy, and after what he'd said, my breath was only just returning to my lungs.

"What?"

He grinned. "Are you satisfied? Satisfied being a

Diamond woman, where you get set up with a man and your life revolves around charity events?"

I puffed out my cheeks, piercing a piece of lobster tail. I poked at it for a while, then dipped it into the cream sauce before putting my fork down.

"Satisfied?" I shrugged. "It's complicated, Barrett."

Opening the salads and putting some on my plate, he said, "Try me."

"Mom's matchmaking… I don't like it, but I understand it."

He raised an eyebrow but stayed silent.

"And I've quit trying to edge my way into working. I floated the idea of maybe one day becoming an editor at my debutante ball, and Connor slammed that idea down. I think you may have been there."

"I was. I remember. So that's it?"

"No, I've mentioned it to Mom and Dad as well over the years."

"Mentioned it? Maybe you should try harder, Lourde. Life is anything but fair."

He outstretched his arms, the sun hit his chest and face, lighting him up like a Greek god of sex.

"Easy for you to say." I ate the next few mouthfuls in silence. How would he know what it was like being a Diamond woman? I swallowed down the food, not caring to chew it. When I looked up, he was staring at me. A pain etched behind his eyes, similar to what I'd seen before.

"Nothing was ever easy for me. My father abused Evelyn and me. He was a violent man. He abused Mom for as long as I could remember. My childhood was anything but easy."

I blinked. The gravity of what he just said hit me. "Barrett. I didn't know. I'm so sorry."

"I don't need your pity, Lourde. I'm telling you this, so

hopefully, you realize if you want something bad enough, grab it by the balls like I did, or life will tear you down. I guarantee it."

"I understand. Does Connor know all of this?"

"Not about the abuse, no. No one knows this but you."

I watched the pain hold in his eyes. "I'm not going to tell anyone, Barrett."

Kids ran past our picnic, and sand kicked up around us.

"Hey, watch it," Barrett said. And the moment we just shared quickly passed by.

"Thank you for telling me," I said, dusting off the sand from the edge of the picnic rug.

"Yeah, well, now we have sandy lobster tails."

"I don't mind," I said, smiling at him.

He smiled back. "Well, we have to eat. Otherwise, we won't have energy for what I want to do to you later."

Why does he do that? Wreck a beautiful moment by turning it into just sex. Minimizing it, so all we have is between the sheets.

Annoyed, I finished my salad in silence, admiring the beautiful sunset—the scent of the ocean, seaweed, and laughter in the distance. Maybe life wasn't fair. Maybe I had to go and claim what I was after, or perhaps I could settle for a man Mom wanted me to marry and not work, not use my brain, but the passion to work, if anything, was growing stronger, and I didn't want my Ivy League education going to waste.

I exhaled, then felt the weight of his stare fall upon me. "You're staring," I said.

His stare lingered, then darkened. "Let's go home."

My body responded, tingling from head to toe. At this moment, I didn't care if he ignored the previous moment we had. The anticipation inside of me brewed, and I couldn't wait any longer for his hands to be on me and inside of me.

"Let's."

The car ride home was short but not so short his hand couldn't trail up my leg, push my scrap of lace aside and finger me until I gripped the leather seat and moaned his name. By the time we made it to the house, I was already a tangled mess.

He followed me into my bedroom, watching me slip out of my yellow sundress, my hair dusting the tips of my shoulders. He leaned against the door frame as I stood in my new lingerie—a scarlet-red corset and satin belt with French lace covering half my ass.

"Leave it on." He stalked over to me, unbuttoning his shirt, and kicked off his shoes.

I stood at the edge of the bed. Slowly, I ran my hand across his muscled, tanned chest. I was too impatient, so I moved his hand, ripping his shirt open. Buttons flew everywhere, landing all over the rug. He widened his eyes, then grinned. "That was my favorite shirt, dollface."

"I'll buy you a new one." I smirked.

"You're going to pay for that but not the way you think." He slipped down his pants, his eyes dark.

"Spread your legs, dollface. I want to taste you until you beg me not to."

"Soon but first…" I bent down, pulled his white briefs down, then wrapped my mouth around his delicious cock, tasting his pre-cum on my lips.

"Fuck, Lourde." He hissed.

I licked his tip, then tongued the length of him. Closing my lips around him, I took him up and down. I was so hot for him. I felt my wetness pool between my legs.

His hands gripped the back of my head. "Fuck," he groaned out, and it only made me hotter. After a beat, he pulled out of my mouth, and I looked up from my knees. *Did he not like it anymore?*

"Dollface, I want to come inside you, and right now, you're going to make me blow like Krakatoa."

Oh.

He lifted me, threw me firmly on my bed, and climbed on top of me. I dragged my hand over his cheek. I wanted to kiss him, taste his lips on mine, but I hesitated. I trailed his neck with kisses before he raked his teeth across my nipple, his touch blistering. My sex clenched.

"It's my turn to taste you."

He trailed my stomach with kisses, his breath hot. I squirmed, relishing every intense sensation. Then he spread apart my legs and, without warning, his tongue dipped inside me. My head shot back into the pillow as I let out a groan. His fingers circled my clit as he took long strokes inside me. Heat slashed my chest as I arched my back.

"Barrett." I breathed as my body released and convulsed around him.

"Fuck, you're perfect," he said, staring at me when I opened my eyes. He took out a condom and wrapped himself, and while I was soaking in his bliss, he dipped into me.

I tipped my head up, and my lips found his. He hesitated for a second, but when our tongues collided, he deepened the kiss. I tasted my sweetness on him. He moved quicker and deeper, fucking me harder. My arm stretched out, grabbing the covers. His arm fell on mine as his hand clasped into my palm, squeezing it tight.

My body burned, igniting within when the connection between us deepened. I eagerly arched my hips up, meeting him, and groaned into his mouth. His tongue delved deeper, consuming me, and that was my undoing.

I quivered as each wave of passion rolled over me. Barrett's pace slowed as he moved, each push and pull with deliberate intention. Then he released a gritty moan as he pushed, deepening our connection and came undone. Resting his forehead on mine, still holding my hand, he opened his eyes. My heart beat erratically as his gaze bored into mine. *Oh my God, what was that?*

I tilted my chin up to kiss him, but he moved away.

"Three for three, dollface. I'm off to bed."

He peeled off me, naked, and walked out the door without looking back.

Suddenly, I went cold. A tightness balled in my chest. I wrapped my arms around my naked body, trying to comprehend what just happened.

21

BARRETT

W *hatever the fuck that was, it wasn't happening again.*
My legs grew heavy as they carried me back to my room. I shut my door, walked over to my bed, and fell onto it, where I stared at the ceiling.

My phone beeped, pulling me from the feeling settling in the pit of my stomach. Turning my phone over, I read the trail of messages from the boys catching up from the last few hours. They were flying in tomorrow night. Magnus declared it, wanting to forget about his missus and organized the boys for a fly-in-and-out trip. *Great.*

I turned to my nightstand. The clock glared, 12:10 a.m. Having Lourde around was becoming way too comfortable, and I'd let my control go wayward. Pleasing her and not only between the sheets was what I wanted to do. In fact, it was all I could think about.

Who the fuck was I turning into?

I didn't even recognize myself anymore. Then I'd divulged the truth about my family, well half of it. I left out the most important part of how my parents died. But I felt compelled to tell her something. Lourde needed to know, like me, she could get everything she ever wanted, especially when it looked like there was no way out, even if we had come from different circumstances and our motivations were completely different.

She had limitless means. I had to support my sister and find her the care she needed from her gunshot wound.

Lourde had a first-class education. I lied to get my foot in the door at a local realtor.

Lourde could do whatever she wanted in life. I hustled, working day and night just to make ends meet and pay Evelyn's medical bills. Commuting from Providence to Manhattan every day for that job led to meeting people like Connor Diamond—the break I needed to start new and build my business. Now hundreds of employees' entire livelihoods depended on me, but I didn't deserve any of it. Just like I didn't deserve Lourde.

Yet, she was the spark, grinding back my sharp edges each day we spent together, making me believe differently. She deserved someone who could treat her right. Someone dependable and from a noteworthy family. Someone without my dark past. I closed my eyes and welcomed the darkness.

* * *

Today I left early, leaving before dawn just to avoid her. I raced through meetings. We got the signed contract with the ten million off—like I knew we would—and all that remained now was due diligence and the legal team to do their thing.

I could've left days ago. But I was still here.

I should be in my office back in Manhattan. But I wasn't. Instead, I was sitting opposite my Vice President of Sales, Lucio, Olivia, my interior designer, and her second in charge, Jessica. All because I summoned them to the Hamptons to discuss the launch of a site in Brooklyn.

I tossed the coin, flipping it over my knuckles repeatedly, then back again. The taste of her lingered on my tongue, and her smile was etched on my mind. If I was any more of a pussy… *Fuck!* I slammed the coin down on the table.

All eyes drew toward me. "Everything okay, Barrett?" Lucio asked as he lowered his glasses.

"Perfect, why?" I glared at Lucio. "Let's just finish up. It's getting late," I said, sliding the plans back across to Olivia.

She regarded me, then took the plans and started rolling them up.

"Right. You heard the man. We'll have the interior decorating of all eight homes complete in two weeks."

She put the elastic band over the plans and stood up. "Lucio, I think we have a plane to catch. If there isn't anything else, Barrett?"

The sun was setting. People were arriving at my house. There wasn't anything else I needed except *her*.

* * *

My phone sounded through the Bose speakers as I drove back to the house. My sister's name flashed up on the dash screen.

"Evelyn. I'm sorry, I should've called you earlier."

"Hey. I understand you've been busy. Congrats on the sale of 21 Park. I knew you could do it."

"Thanks, sis. When that completes, I've got a condo in Soho with your name on it."

"Plus, the 21 Park apartment and my house in Boston? Stop buying me real estate, Barrett!"

"Not going to happen, sis. I've always got your back."
If I bought enough real estate in Manhattan, maybe she
could move here.

"How many times do I have to tell you, Barrett? I'm
happy in Boston."

"But I don't get to see you that much."

"I know, but I'm happy here."

"How's physical therapy going after the operation?"

"Slow, but I feel more and more each day since."

"I'm so pleased you've got some movement back after
the last operation. You know I'll help get you whatever you
need. Just tell me, and it's yours."

"You know I will. Tell me, how are you? Still bedding
anything that walks?"

I laughed too loudly for my own ears.

"Wait. Have you met someone, Barrett?"

"Lourde Diamond has been staying with me in the
Hamptons' house. Long story."

"As in Connor Diamond's sister, Lourde?"

"Yes." I swallowed. *What the heck was I doing?*

"She's a gorgeous girl, Barrett. But I don't need to tell
you, you're in dangerous territory there."

"I know. Anyway, she has a date with her future
husband on Friday night." I cleared my throat. "So this
little thing we had going on is ending, which is probably a
good thing."

"Then why don't you seem pleased?"

I didn't have an answer, and it wasn't any clearer as I
pulled into my drive.

"Hello?"

"Sis, I've got to go. I've just arrived at the house, and
I'm hosting a party tonight. And I think all the boys are
here already."

"This conversation isn't over, Barrett."

"Talk soon."

"Barrett—"

I hung up and inhaled, my lungs suddenly depleted of oxygen.

* * *

When I first got home, I said a quick hello before darting upstairs to change out of my suit and into casual pants and a black t-shirt. I noticed Lourde's door was closed, so I returned downstairs.

Hunkholes? Was that what Lourde had called the four of us?

Connor, Ari, and Magnus sat on the deck drinking and eating whatever the caterers provided. People mingled and chatted in the living room. Mostly, I knew all of them. I was getting used to having people in the house, and the little things didn't seem to bother me as much.

The boys drank Hennessy, and I cracked a beer.

"This view sucks, Barrett," Ari said, staring out toward the black, endless ocean. The sun had set, the moon had risen, and a yellow line reflected off of the ocean's surface.

"Yeah, it does." I elbowed him.

"So, to what do I owe this occasion, fellas? I feel like I've seen way too much of you guys lately."

"I need to fuck and party, maybe not in that order," Magnus said, downing his drink, then pouring another straight from the bottle.

"Your dick's not going to work if you keep that up," Connor said, tipping his head at his now refilled glass.

"You know it's a Wednesday, right?" I inquired.

"It's party night any night in the Hamptons, especially since my wife's had another dick in her." Magnus held up his glass in the center of our group.

"Agreed." I toasted him.

"I'm with you, bud," Connor said, toasting him before clinking glasses with me. Guilt washed over me.

"Let's party," Ari added.

We all took a sip of our drinks, then Connor turned to me and asked, "Where's Lourde?"

"Beats me," I said, taking the beer to my lips again.

The summer breeze cooled the recent heat that slashed upward from my neck. Since when did I ever need to evade a conversation?

Connor threw me a scowl, his blue eyes asking for a truth I didn't want to give him.

Where was she, anyway? Wherever she was, I knew she hated me for what I did to her last night. Fucking her was different last night. Things changed when I divulged a bit about my past, and our hands met and remained clasped when we both came.

Bad luck, dollface. You knew I was an asshole. I never lied about that.

I watched as he took out his phone, putting it to his ear for a moment before hanging up. His scowl returned. "She's not answering." I pretended not to hear and chimed in on Magnus and Ari's conversation about football, which I knew nothing about.

"Who are they?" Connor's scowl disappeared as he eye-fucked one of four women strutting toward us.

"Gentlemen." A leggy blonde woman, the same one Connor had been staring at, approached and stood beside him. Her friends joined in around us.

"Chelsea, so nice to see you," Ari said, kissing her cheeks. "This is my friend, Magnus, I wanted you to meet." Magnus' eyes lit up, and I guarantee you any thoughts of his ex-soon disappeared.

"And this is Ciara, Peach, and Madison." Damn, they

all looked like *Sports Illustrated* models—leggy, titty, gorgeous. But my dick wasn't responding.

"Fancy a walk along the beach?" Magnus asked Chelsea, then stood, a little uneasily on his feet.

"Jesus, Magnus, at least get the girl a drink first," Ari said, shaking his head.

"It's okay, Ari," Chelsea said. "I'd love to, Magnus." She linked arms with him as they walked off, likely to fuck.

Ari puffed out his cheeks. "Girls, let me introduce you to Barrett and Connor."

"You wouldn't also be the Barrett who owns this stunning home?" A redhead asked, siding up next to me.

"He is," Connor added while gesturing the blonde—Ciara—to sit on his lap.

"Hey, I'm Madison." While she wanted me to smile and be polite, I didn't. I was an asshole.

"Hey."

Ciara was already sitting on Connor, laughing about fuck knows what while stroking his chest. Peach and Ari looked like they were moments away from fucking, even though they'd just met.

A hand fell on my shoulder. "Feel like company, Barrett?" I glanced up at her, and she looked down at me expectantly.

Ignoring her, I leaned over to Ari. "Were you in charge of the guest list?"

"Yeah, and aren't you thanking me now?" He squeezed the ass of the woman on him, and she giggled.

I rolled my eyes, and he narrowed his. "Or is there someone else you're waiting for?"

A strangled laugh left my lips. "Sure, gorgeous." I took her hand and dragged her to my lap, at the same time staring Ari down.

22

LOURDE

It was so obvious now. I was just a fuck to him, nothing more. I watched as a redhead draped herself over him, his broad shoulders and back facing me as I walked down the stairs. I'd have doubled over in pain if people hadn't already seen me.

Politely, I chatted with the few familiar faces that came up. Then, removing myself as quickly as possible, I walked over to the kitchen counter, and I helped myself to the tray of canapes, emotionally eating one after the other.

In the late afternoon, when Connor rang, I was shopping with the girls. He said Barrett was hosting another party, and they were flying in tonight. Caterers and party planners were at the house by the time I arrived, and I hid in my room, deciding I needed space from Barrett after last night. But as the music and laughter echoed up the stairs and the missed call from Connor, I thought I should make an appearance. *Heck, why should they have all the fun?*

The coconut shrimp danced on my taste buds, and I ate three more. Peering through the crowd, I could just make out Ari and Connor chatting with their dates, but my gaze fixed firmly on that dark mane of thick hair and the gorgeous woman playing with it.

Who the fuck was she?

My throat clogged with emotion while my skin burned with rage. Suddenly, my feet moved from the spot where I was standing in the kitchen as the adrenaline pointed me toward their table. He was my brother. I'd have to say hello. If I didn't at least say a brief hello, I knew he'd pester me until he knew where I was.

Wearing a white shirt-dress with my lace emerald bra poking through, I steadied my needle heels against the floor as I moved from the kitchen to the living room.

I didn't really recognize anyone. Ari had fashion connections from his late grandmother's fashion house that still ran today, and Connor knew everyone from Manhattan to the Hamptons, so getting a last-minute crowd together on billionaires' row wasn't difficult.

"Connor!" I exclaimed, hardly recognizing my high-pitched voice.

"Sis!" He peered up from his seat and smiled. He tapped the woman on his lap, and she stood up quickly. He shot up to hug me, then released me. "You're sunburned," he frowned.

"This?" I pointed to my body. "It's so much better."

"Lourde, aren't you a breath of fresh air?" Ari said, coming over. He kissed me on both cheeks.

Barrett was trying to get up when I said, "Stay. You both look busy anyway."

I didn't even look at him. I couldn't look at him. He made zero effort to show remorse, let alone say hello.

"What can I get you, sis?" Connor asked.

"I can't stay."

"You just got here," Connor said.

The gorgeous woman whispered something in Barrett's

ear, and nerves shot up my spine. Anger coursed through my veins, filling them with lead.

"I promised someone I'd go for a walk with him along the beach."

What the?

In the corner of my eye, I noticed Barrett sit up straighter.

"Hang on a minute, who?" Connor asked.

"Just a friend," I said, letting my lips curl into a smirk.

"Someone's moved on quickly." Ari laughed.

"Oh, I have." My voice was deadly serious, hoping to get a rise out of Barrett.

"Barrett, have you met this friend?" Connor asked.

"Can't say I have." I met Barrett's steely gaze. His jaw set into a razor-sharp line. In a show of strength, I straightened, lifting my chin. Two could play at this game.

I'll show you that not all women are affected by Barrett Black. I can forget you just like you forgot me.

"Well, I'd like to meet him before you leave, okay?" My brother looked at me. Concern etched across his face.

Fuck. "Sure, I'll just go get him."

I caught Barrett's eye just before turning. Darkness burned behind his dark greens. I smiled politely before retreating.

Walking inside and toward the living room, it didn't take long to spot a gorgeous man.

"Hey, I'm Lourde. I have a favor to ask."

"I know who you are. I'm Michael."

Tall, fair, and shaggy brown hair, Michael looked at me with daring eyes.

"Yeah, no, it's not like that."

"Oh." He frowned.

"It's going to sound weird, but can we go for a walk along the beach, or at least pretend we're going to? Before we do that, though, we have to meet my brother and his friends over there, and I need you to pretend you're into me."

He looked from me toward the balcony where throngs of people now congregated. "Well, if it means I get to walk along the beach with Lourde Diamond, sure."

I rolled my eyes. "Hey, there's no funny business." God, even Barrett's words were rubbing off on me.

"Can't say I won't try." He tossed me a grin, and I laughed.

"Michael!"

He crooked his arm, and I took it in mine. "Thank you," I said.

We walked from the foyer toward the deck, then through the living room area when he turned. Barrett's gaze collided with mine, then breaking it, his gaze fell on my hand in Michael's.

I straightened my back. "Connor, meet Michael."

Michael extended his arm. "Connor, nice to meet you."

Connor looked at him, respectable in his crisp white shirt, tailored pants, and loafers. Connor gave him a once over.

"Join us for a drink?"

"Sure," Michael said, taking the empty seat next to Connor.

No! That wasn't part of the plan.

"I think we'll just go for a stroll first," I said.

"Nonsense," Barrett said, getting up. As he did, his woman was unsteady but regained her balance. He dragged the chair next to his. "Lourde, here you go." He patted the chair, and I walked past him, brushing his legs as he sat back down. Nerves shot up my spine. Images of him between my legs danced in my mind.

"Ari, grab that one for Michael, is it?" Barret asked.

"Thanks," he said.

I sat as conversation swirled around me. Michael was confident around the men, even knowing a few people that Ari knew. Barrett's missus for the night excused herself and walked around him, heading inside the house.

I toyed with my tasseled belt cinched around my shirt-dress, watching Connor banter with my new friend. It turns out Michael was a respectable lawyer, something my brother would approve of. My ears pricked when Michael asked Barrett about Diamond Incorporated.

After a while, Michael turned to me. "And what do you do in the media business, Lourde?"

I opened my mouth to speak, but Connor spoke first. "Lourde? Nothing, she doesn't want to be a part of it."

"I think Michael was asking Lourde the question. Wasn't he, Connor?" There was a slightly odd expression coming from Connor as he and Barrett looked at one another.

"Of course, she can. Sorry, sis."

Well, that was new. Barrett standing up for me and in front of my brother?

Barrett's focus fell upon me, his gaze lingering on mine. My gaze flickered between Connor and Barrett.

"Not yet. But one day, I'd like to." I focused on my brother. His perplexed look carried over to me.

"God knows why? The amount of pressure I'm under with Dad and the board breathing down my neck."

"I can help you, Connor."

"Maybe she ought to," Ari said.

"Shut up, Ari," Connor snapped.

"Even if I wanted you there, sis, Mother would never allow it. You know that. Now, let's just give it a rest. I came here to relax for the night."

He stared at the woman on his lap. She only had one

thing on her mind. In fact, they all did. I couldn't bear to think of Barrett inside another woman. I glanced at him as I shied away from the conversation. He put his drink on the table and turned to me. "Don't play with me, dollface." His voice was gravelly, low.

I peered around, making sure no one was listening. Ari glanced momentarily our way before returning his attention to his woman.

"You're the one playing," I said firmly. I watched his chest rise and fall. He was just as angry and infuriated as I was. *But why?* He'd started it all.

"Meet me upstairs, *now.*"

What? How?

"Do it," he reiterated.

"Excuse me while I find my girl. I'm randier than a teenage dick," Barrett announced to the table.

I choked on my champagne. Connor laughed loudly. So did Ari. "Barrett, not in front of Lourde. Geez!"

"Sorry, Lourde, I forgot you were there. You're just like one of the boys sometimes."

He excused himself and pushed out his seat. My eyes caught a glimmer of his curved tight ass.

Now what?

What was I meant to say to remove myself and Michael?

"Shall we go for a walk now?" I asked my new friend.

I looked to Connor, who smiled, giving me the silent okay that this guy was good enough for his baby sister. "Come back soon, sis."

"Of course." I flashed him my most innocent smile.

"Nice to meet you, Michael," Connor said.

"Likewise, Connor," he replied, and we walked around the table toward the back stairs.

"Your brother seems nice."

"If you mean overprotective, then yeah, I guess. I have another favor to ask."

He laughed, looking out toward the sea. "Can we walk out toward the beach so they can see us, then double back to the house really quick? Then if you can just be out of sight from my brother for like half an hour, that would be great."

"You're shady, Lourde." I shrugged. "Only if you promise me if it doesn't work out with whomever this guy is that has your attention, you call me next."

I smiled again. He was all right. It wouldn't hurt. "Deal," I said.

We walked out along the boardwalk, my brother, Ari, and their women behind us. As soon as our feet hit the sand, we walked back alongside the house, around the front, arriving at the front door.

"I hope he's worth it," Michael said, kissing me on the cheek.

"So do I."

23

BARRETT

I waited in the darkness in her room for what felt like fucking forever.

Politely, I'd excused myself from the attractive woman draped over me. The same woman I was using as a pawn to make Lourde jealous. I didn't play games. That wasn't me. So then, why did I want to pretend I was going to sleep with the woman on my lap? Sure, there was the keeping up appearances aspect so her brother wouldn't be led astray, thinking something was going on between Lourde and me. But it was more than that. I was angry.

Maybe it was because she ignored me, only greeting her brother and politely acknowledging Ari. It was definitely because she'd said she was taking a walk along the beach with someone.

I was breaking her down piece by piece. Like I broke everything and anyone around me. I had to break her to protect her. She deserved better than me. She deserved a life with someone worthy of giving her a life who cared for her. Not a monster like me.

I took a life—the life dearest to my own. My mother

was lying in a Providence cemetery because I couldn't wrestle the gun. My sister, permanently disabled because a bullet hit a nerve in her upper thigh, affecting her walking.

Like the monster I was, I hid. In Lourde's room, in the dark. Behind the door. I wanted her to find me. Bring light to my dark heart if only for the brief moments we shared.

Footsteps sounded across the floor. Then the door pushed open, and she stepped in. Lit up by the moon's light, her shadow casting across the wall. Before she could turn the light on, I grabbed her and pinned her against the door, shutting it.

She gasped but didn't object.

In the gray room, I could make her out. Every expression, every angle on her porcelain skin, and her eyes bored into mine.

"Where's your date?" she asked in a whisper.

"I don't give a fuck." I'd cornered a rich colleague and asked him to occupy her for the next hour away from the boys before sending her home. That way, Connor and the boys wouldn't suspect anything.

"Jealous?" I tilted my head, and she blinked rapidly. The column of her neck sucked inward.

She was.

Her hands trembled underneath the force of mine, pinning her against the door with my body. My erection lengthened along my seam.

"No, you're just an asshole."

She'd driven me mad with that man—hooked in each other's arms. I watched how his hand fell on hers, and he didn't belong anywhere near her. She was mine.

"You're the one parading with a man on your arm," I said, roughly kissing her neck.

She moaned. "He's a nice man who wanted to walk me along the beach."

"*Nice.*"

"Yes," she replied on an exhale.

"Nice like this?" Sliding one hand down her front, I lifted her dress and pushed her underwear to the side. She was ready for me. I slid two fingers inside of her.

"Who's jealous now?" She groaned, taking her mouth to my ear. Her breath was warm, and my pulse raced. This was beyond dangerous, but I had to have her. My lips found her mouth, swallowing her words. Our tongues thrashed about, desperately claiming one another.

I pulled back and stared her in the eyes. "I don't get jealous, dollface. Now slide over and kiss the wall. This is going to be hard and fast."

Rage and lust burned behind her hazels. Before turning, she paused. I unzipped my pants, freeing my bulging cock. I pushed her hair to the side and trailed the nape of her neck with rough kisses. Tossing up her dress, I pushed her panties to the side, not bothering to remove them, and rubbed my tip at her entrance. I dipped inside of her, stretching her with each stroke. "Fuck, Lourde." I hissed, feeling her wetness.

Angrily, I plowed into her, one stroke after the other. She took it, all of me, her body pressed against the wall.

"You're not a nice person, Barrett." She moaned, her face still turned to the side.

I pressed my lips against her ear. "Yet you want to scream my name, dollface," I said with a harsh whispered tone.

"No, I don't." Her voice trembled with false denial.

Needing to prove a point, I wrapped my hand around the front of her neck, gently applying pressure. "Don't lie to me," I warned.

"It hurts to want you," she said, her voice strained as she breathed out.

Her words hit me square in the chest. I didn't want to hurt her—Lourde, of all people.

Quickly, I turned her around. She stared at me, not giving anything away. The noise from outside the room floated and ate at the silence between us. I kissed her on the mouth. Slowly, sensually, giving her a taste of what she deserved. I spread her legs and lifted her with one arm, her back against the wall. Her legs found their way around my hips. Her hands wrapped around my neck and up through my hair.

She tipped her head back and groaned loudly after I thrust into her. I watched her moan. The long column of her neck. The way her tits bounced up and down against my chest at each thrust. A strange feeling inside my chest hit me. She pulled back off the wall, her eyes collided with mine, her hair fell around the sides of her face, her fruity floral fragrance overwhelming all my senses.

I pushed into her further. I was close, and so was she. Her lips found mine, and a long, slow breathless kiss tipped me over the edge. "Lourde!" I hissed on a breath riding the waves. A few seconds later, the walls of her cunt pulsed around me as she found her release.

Almost immediately, her legs fell from my waist, and she pulled her dress down. There was something behind her eyes I hadn't seen before.

"I can't see you anymore, Barrett," she croaked out.

And as those words hit me, I came back down to earth, crashing through the floor.

"I know."

* * *

The next morning, I hung back, waiting for Ari, Magnus, and Connor to wake, then leave. But really, I was waiting for her.

I pushed my meeting to later in the day.

"What a night," Magnus stated, satisfied he'd gotten his dick wet.

You disappeared early," Ari said, sipping his espresso and staring at me.

"Well, you know me." I grinned.

'Where's Lourde? We have to go now, and she's still not up," Connor inquired.

"Maybe she had a busy night!" Ari grinned. "That guy seemed nice."

A vein throbbed in my neck. Connor shot me a look. "What?"

"We have that family dinner on Friday, where Mom and Dad have Senator Connolly coming over with his son, who's more suitable."

"Why is he more suitable than Michael?" I asked.

Connor's phone rang, so I wasn't sure how much he took in my question, which was probably a good thing seeing it was none of my damn business anyway.

"Oh, no," Ari said, staring at me.

"Oh, he did," Magnus added.

Shit.

"Tell me you were fucking the woman on your lap and not Lourde."

"I was fucking the woman on my lap." I deadpanned.

"Barrett, are you fucking crazy? Lourde is their princess. If Connor finds out, he'll crucify you."

"She is eight years younger than you," Magnus added.

"Yeah, well, so fucking what."

"Don't pretend you don't care. She's not someone you just fuck," Ari spat.

"Yes, she is." I shrugged. "She wanted a taste of freedom, so I gave it to her. Now I'm going back to Manhattan, and she's got a suitor to charm and fall in love with. It was a one-time thing."

"You're so fucked, my friend, I can't even…" Magnus added. "And here I was thinking I had fucking problems with my cheating wife. Ha! You're in a world of more pain than me."

You don't know the half of it.

"No, I'm not, and I don't give a fuck what Connor says. But it would be best for you two to keep your mouths shut unless you want this to come between us."

"Fuck, I'm not saying a word," Magnus said.

"Yeah, are you crazy?" Ari agreed.

Connor snapped off his phone call, and I watched him walk back inside from the balcony. "Right, we have to go," he said.

I sucked back the rest of my coffee. "Well, boys, I'll see you back in Manhattan soon. My work is done here." I glared at Magnus and Ari.

"Well, come to dinner on Friday if you're around. Meet the guy we want Lourde to fall in love with and live happily ever after."

Both Magnus and Ari laughed. Ari spilled the rest of his coffee on his arm.

I glared at them. "Am I missing something?" Connor asked, picking up his overnight bag.

"No," Magnus said.

"Don't think I'll make it this week, but thanks," I replied. One night was enough seeing Lourde on someone's arm. Another whole evening would be torture. Plus, she said she didn't want to see me anymore. My skin crawled at the thought.

"Tell Lourde I said goodbye," Connor said.

"Sure thing."

* * *

It was after ten o'clock when she surfaced, slowly walking down the stairs. I'm sure she thought I was long gone. But, from the look on her face when she hit the bottom step and spotted me in the kitchen, I think she wished I wasn't here.

Her eyes were puffy. *Had she been crying?*

"Morning," I greeted.

She walked over to the coffee machine, put a cup under, and pressed the button.

"I thought you'd be gone," she blankly stated.

"Sorry to disappoint you."

The air in the room was heavy. She reared up against the corner of the kitchen cabinets, her face strained. "Tell me something, Barrett."

"Shoot."

"Have you ever loved someone?"

What the fuck. "Of course."

"Other than family."

Fuck.

"Thought so. Why is that?"

I shook my head. *Because I'm a monster and don't deserve love.*

"I'm an asshole. I told you that."

She took her coffee from underneath the coffee machine and put the cup to her lips.

"You're right. You're the one who's been absolutely truthful and upfront."

She slammed the coffee down so hard it left a scratch on the counter. "But you say you're an asshole, then you kiss me as if you want me all to yourself, organize picnics, and rub lotion on me like you care. You even stood up to Connor when no one stands up to my brother. All those things don't add up to being an asshole."

Heat slashed my neck. I hadn't even realized I'd done all those things until just then.

She looked at me. "This has been fun. We have been fun. But I want more."

"Last night, you said we were done."

"We are unless you can give me what I deserve."

"And what is that?"

"Love."

I swallowed. Every muscle tensed at her honesty. "I can't give you that, Lourde."

"Why?" Her voice was quiet.

"It doesn't matter why."

"It does to me."

Her voice trembled, and something inside of me broke, but I had to steady myself. I couldn't be the man she deserved.

"Because I don't love you." Suddenly, my ribs felt too tight, pulling inward and sucking the air from my lungs.

She blinked back tears and pushed away her coffee, her hand trembling. "I see." She turned and walked to the stairs, picking up her packed bag I hadn't noticed. "Well, goodbye, Barrett."

I let her walk away.

Watching her as she walked down the hallway and opened the door to the waiting car, she didn't look back. I felt like I'd been sucker-punched in the ribs, and I didn't fucking understand it.

24

LOURDE

I'd already cried enough tears over Barrett Black by the time my driver had dropped me back home. Pepper and Grace had helped me get through the painful journey home from the Hamptons and listened to me on the phone talking about the man who had somehow stolen my heart in the space of a week. But as Pepper had said, it wasn't a week at all. I'd known Barrett for way longer, and what started as an innocent one-sided crush years ago had developed into something I don't think either of us expected.

But it was over.

He couldn't give me what I wanted. It seemed he wasn't capable of love.

I said a quick hello to Mom, then escaped to my bedroom, pulling the covers over my head like the emptiness I felt was a bad dream. But when I awoke, that feeling was there. Worse still, I had a throbbing headache and an insatiable hunger from not eating since last night.

I pulled myself together, patted some concealer on my puffy eyes, and went downstairs to meet Mom for lunch.

"Here she is." She lifted her head and took me in. "Lourde, you look terrible, darling."

"I have a headache, Mom, that's all."

"And a terrible sunburn. You should really let our doctor look at that. You don't want that beautiful skin of yours to peel, although…" she laughed, "… that's what we want when we get to my age… the skin underneath, the new, peeled layers." She pulled her cheeks toward her ears.

I shook my head at the taut expression on Mom's face. "Barrett called the concierge doctor in the Hamptons. I have this cream, he… I mean, I apply daily." I blushed, remembering the feel of his large hands rubbing the cream into my neck, then circling my breasts.

"Is that so?" She ran her eyes over me as I slid onto the chair beside her.

"Yes." I dug into the Waldorf salad, my favorite.

"How was it at Barrett's?" Mom asked, picking at the lettuce in her Greek salad.

"His house is beautiful, Mom, so full of character, detail, and the view… just stunning."

That's it, stick to the house.

"I remember when he bought that house. We were so perplexed by it. It was so rundown and old. And Barrett?"

"Barrett was working a lot on a deal in East Hampton."

"Always working, Barrett. So you didn't see him much?"

"Not really." I couldn't help but lie.

"Hmm. He's very good-looking."

I turned to Mom. A grin spread onto her mouth as she regarded me.

I laughed. "I guess he is."

"You guess?"

"Can we change the topic?" I shoveled more chicken in my mouth so that I couldn't engage in conversation anymore.

"Tomorrow night. How are you feeling about meeting Finigan?"

Eventually, I swallowed. "To be honest, Mom, I don't want to date so soon."

"Nonsense. We've been through this before. You're not getting any younger, Lourde, and Finigan is quite the catch."

I shook my head. "Like Hunter was?" I glared at her. "I saw him with his dick in another woman on the beach, Mom."

"Lourde! Language, please."

I rolled my eyes. I'll always be the debutante in her eyes.

"Men are a different species. They think with their…" she looked down. *Could she not say cock?*

"Cocks?"

"Lourde, what has gotten into you?"

When I didn't respond, she continued, "They think with their appendages sometimes. I believe Hunter really cared for you. He just had a lapse in judgment."

"You can't be serious, Mom."

"Men have them, dear, especially powerful men." She held my gaze, and something behind her normally calm exterior wavered. Was she referring to her and Dad? They had always been in a solid, loving relationship.

"All I'm saying is to be open tomorrow night. Finigan is a sweet boy, and he comes from an excellent family, Lourde. They're scarce these days."

I picked at the feta Mom had left in her salad bowl. "Maybe, Mom."

* * *

All afternoon, Mom had begged me to help her pick an outfit for this evening. We'd spent the last few hours in and out of shops. Still unhappy, she got her stylist to pick a few pieces up and deliver them to the house. She'd even organized a few for me to try.

I settled on a royal blue dress, cinched in the waist and flaring to the knee. Pairing it with my Yves Saint Laurent nude pumps would work wonderfully.

It was nice to get dressed up for a change and put on some makeup. Hamptons' wear was uber casual, and I hadn't worn a full face of makeup the entire time I was there. I looked at my reflection in the mirror. All I could see was Barrett with his hands on my body, his legs between mine, and his taste on my tongue. Since yesterday, I'd hidden in my room hoping to rid Barrett from my mind until Mom dragged me out shopping today, but I couldn't stop thinking about him.

"Ready!" Mom burst into my room on the other side of the house.

She donned a stunning Georgian lace dress with embellished shoulder detail. For a woman who just turned fifty, she looked stunning. I'm sure the monthly visits from Dr. Castle may have had something to do with that.

"You look beautiful, Mom."

"Oh, darling. Look at you. You'll make a beautiful bride someday. Front of the paper for you, sweetheart."

I wanted to say, is that because we own the papers but instead, I settled for, "Thanks, Mom."

"What's wrong?" She remained standing, not daring to sit down and get her dress wrinkled before the main event.

"I'm just not at all excited about this evening." And I

kept replaying my time with Barrett over and over in my head like a torture wheel.

"I know, I know. But trust me on this one. Finigan is very handsome and intelligent, and comes from a well-regarded family."

"I know he is."

"You do?"

I nodded. Well, of course, I googled the man I was being set up with, and truth be told, he was extremely handsome, my age, and tall—just my type. The problem was, I'd tasted dirty and dark and craved it like a drug. I wanted that. I wanted Barrett.

"Good. Great, then enjoy yourself tonight. The Hamptons can wait for their princess."

I smiled. "Thanks, Mom, but I'm not sure I'll be going back."

On the ride back, I told Pepper and Grace I wouldn't be returning. I needed time to get over everything that had happened. And even though they were bummed, they understood.

"Oh, why?"

Because I've fallen for a man who doesn't love me, and it's just too damn painful to see him again.

"Just want to hang here for a while." I admired my chignon bun in the mirror, trying to throw Mom off the scent.

"Excellent. Well, I'll tell Finigan of your change of plans."

Wonderfuckingful.

"Come on. Let's go downstairs. Your brother and Barrett have probably arrived."

I stopped. "What?" My voice came out in a shout.

She turned her head, pausing at the threshold. "Is that a problem?"

Quickly, I regained my composure. "No, not at all. I just thought he was in the Hamptons."

"He said he had to pop back for something urgent and bumped into your brother, who invited him tonight. Now come along. It's not like a Diamond to keep anyone waiting."

Fuck.

25

BARRETT

T he Hamptons deal was signed, sealed, and delivered. My team was celebrating around the boardroom table on the twenty-ninth floor in the building I owned in midtown while I watched with a sick feeling at the base of my stomach.

Why hadn't I put up a fight when Connor asked me around for dinner tonight? I'd practically invited myself too, knowing full well I'd be witnessing Lourde vying for another man's affections right in front of me.

I felt like fucking roadkill just before impact. I'd intentionally shut Lourde out, admitting I didn't see her in my future. I did it for her. I did it all for her. But that sickening feeling in the pit of my stomach hadn't left since she walked out on me two days ago. It had only gotten worse. Boozy nights since have been made worse by thundering hangovers. Happiness should pour out of me after securing the Hamptons' deal of the century. But it was the opposite. I was a fucking nightmare.

"Boss, have a drink with us. You should celebrate."

Olivia left her interior design team and walked over. I hadn't even noticed her beside me until she spoke.

"Not now, Olivia," I said.

She took that as an invitation to sit down. *Fuck.*

"What's going on, Barrett? Ever since you've been back, you've been... well, if I can be blunt, an ass. Even at the Hamptons, you seemed distracted."

I looked over at her, surprised by her admission. Olivia was always upfront. That's why I'd hired her. But never *that* upfront. Straightforward and brilliant, she was one of the few people who stood up to me, and I respected her for that. Plus, she didn't have a boner for me like most other girls in the office.

"Well, that's blunt. But you know I'm an ass." I took a sip of the sparkling water. "I just have a lot going on, is all."

"You have been an even bigger ass."

I lowered my gaze in a warning shot.

"This hasn't got to do with a woman, does it?"

I laughed. "Yeah, you're not going there."

"Oh! It does?"

"No," I snapped, shutting her down immediately.

Confusion etched across her face. "Well, then, if it's not a girl, it wouldn't have something to do with that detective who was loitering around in the lobby earlier?"

I gripped the base of my chair. "What detective?"

"Didn't your PA tell you?"

"No. I told Aimee not to interrupt me today and hold all my meetings." I'd had the occasional detective around the office before, asking questions about an investor who turned out to be indicted for money laundering. But none since then.

Quickly, I scanned my messages, but I couldn't see

anything from my Aimee. I tried calling her, but she had already left for the day.

Hi, you've reached Aimee Wiles from ZF Constructions. Please leave a message.

"Aimee, call me back. It's urgent." I slammed the phone down.

"I'm sure it's nothing," Olivia said.

"Or it's something."

"Maybe someone murdered someone at 21 Park, and they need the ventilation plans because they hid the body in the air shaft."

I laughed, but the levity was short-lived as the image of my mother's lifeless body came flooding in. I shook it away." Let's hope not." I gathered my things. I couldn't be here anymore. "Will you do me a favor, Olivia?"

"Sure."

"Keep the party going, keep everyone happy. Take them out to Nobu. I can't stay. I have somewhere I need to be."

"Oh, fabulous! Sure thing, boss, enjoy yourself." She stood up, grabbed her champagne flute, then threw me a wink.

"It's not like that, Olivia."

She waved me away with her hand and walked back over to the team.

* * *

"Don't you look stunning, Elizabeth," I greeted, knowing full well that's exactly what she wanted to hear when she entered the room. "Barrett, you're too kind," she said, smiling.

I was early. Intentionally, of course. I needed to see

Lourde and know she was okay. I hadn't expected to be in the company of her parents, Elizabeth and Alfred Diamond, with Connor just making an appearance a few minutes ago.

"Did you close the deal in the Hamptons?" Connor walked in, right on cue.

"Yes, but it wasn't without a bit of drama," I said.

Alfred lowered the rim of his glasses. The lines absent from his wife's face were abundant on his. The twenty-year age gap was more obvious than ever. "How so, Barrett?"

"I secured a hotel in East Hampton, but it wasn't smooth sailing."

"Anything worth anything is damn hard."

Like your daughter.

He took a sip of his whiskey. "So, did it work out?"

"Yes. After my team discovered missing dollars off the bottom line, I went for the jugular."

"Ha! Well done." He held up his glass, congratulating me. "Bet they were pissed."

"You could say that."

"What are we talking about?" Connor said, sipping his overfilled whiskey with a sour scowl on his face.

Alfred rolled his eyes. "Connor's a bit overworked at the minute."

"Absolutely, I am," he said, throwing back a hefty sip.

"Darling, slow down. We can't have you drunk before Governor Connolly arrives. Speaking of which, where did Lourde disappear to? I thought she was right behind me."

"I'm here, Mom." She walked into the sitting room, her beauty bowling me over like a wave. She stole the breath from my lungs. Wearing a royal blue halter neck dress, pulled in at the waist, her hair up, wispy strands framing her face, she was timeless.

Her eyes collided with mine before she tore them away. Behind them lay a pain I was all too familiar with.

Damn, these feelings are real as fuck.

"Good evening, all," she said with a quiet and demure elegance. "Don't you look stunning," Alfred said, admiring his only daughter.

With my free hand, I gripped the side of the chair. A wave of nausea passed over me.

What the fuck?

"Connor, Dad..." she paused. "Barrett."

"She does," I said, agreeing with Alfred.

She blinked before turning and sitting next to her mother on the armchair.

"Right, well, let's try to enjoy ourselves tonight, shall we? This is a wonderful opportunity for Lourde to meet a very handsome man who I think is perfect for her."

I stared at Lourde, but she didn't look up. Instead, she kept her focus on the floor.

"Elizabeth, why don't we let Lourde decide for once. I know James Connolly is a friend of mine, but that doesn't mean his son, Finigan, is perfect for our Lourde here."

We all turned to the man of the house as he took us in. "Well, I'm not lying, am I?"

Elizabeth nearly choked on her martini. "Alfie, please."

"She's still young, for God's sake."

"She needs to be with someone who'll be suitable for her," Connor said, taking his mother's side.

Why couldn't I be that someone?

"Just stop it, all of you, please," Lourde pleaded in a whisper.

The housekeeper walked in, diverting Elizabeth's attention." Your guests have arrived. Shall I show them into the dining room, Mrs. Diamond?"

"Yes, Estelle, please."

Elizabeth finished her martini and hastily walked past

her husband. Connor and Lourde walked out, leaving me with Alfred.

"Are you all right?" I asked.

After a moment, he lifted his head. "I feel for Lourde sometimes. I know what it feels like to be rushed into something."

I was pretty good at reading people, and from the outset, I didn't think it was all roses and fairy dust between Alfie and Lizzy. I'd bet a million dollars he was referring to his own marriage.

"I see."

"How was she with you in the Hamptons, Barrett?" He looked up, and the care in his eyes was something I'd never known but all I ever wanted from my father.

"She was okay. I think she feels trapped sometimes. Especially seeing she's tried over the years to consider working, and she feels like she hasn't been heard."

He pressed his glasses back up the rim of his nose. "It's always been Connor and Elizabeth not wanting her to work. She is so intelligent. You know, sometimes I feel like she'd do a better job than Connor."

His comment floored me.

"Not that you'd ever tell him that, would you, Barrett?"

"I didn't hear it."

"Good answer."

"Come on, let's go before they see us as rude."

"After you."

* * *

Rage bubbled under the surface watching Finigan flirt with Lourde, all right in front of my eyes.

Silently, it built as I watched her talk politics, architecture, and worldly events from entrée through to dessert.

She was the girl that screamed my name and clawed my back with her nails. Not this demure little thing Finigan wanted her to be. What everyone wanted her to be.

With each laugh and each touch she and Finigan shared, it was like a slash to the chest. And what was worse, the guy wasn't actually that bad, so, of course, Lourde was intrigued. Then there was the fact the fuckhead could be Zac Efron's twin.

I hated him.

26

LOURDE

I thought he didn't care, but I was wrong. It was in his wayward glances and subtly in his rigid body when I made the slightest touch on Finigan's arm or laughed at what he'd said.

Barrett fucking cared. A lot.

He looked tired but oh so devilishly handsome too, in his charcoal suit, dark windswept hair, and clean-shaven. Just perhaps the last two days for him had been similarly hellish like mine.

I dipped into my crème brûlé with raspberry compote, enjoying Finigan's company.

He was actually a nice guy. Not that I should be surprised—they all start off that way. However, I couldn't help but half-listen to Finigan while watching Barrett. Not that Finigan noticed. I was the master of social skills, born and raised that way. And a woman could definitely do more than one thing at a time.

His parents were lovely too, talking about their trip to Cannes and his current stint as Governor of Massachusetts. But as the night was coming to an end, sitting opposite Barrett was testing my will.

I knew he cared, but I needed to know if he'd risk it all for me. For love, for what I deserved. Over dessert, I became extra touchy-feely with Finigan, wanting to show Barrett exactly what he'd passed up.

"Another," Connor said to the waiter.

"Connor, don't you think that's enough?" I overheard Barrett ask.

"I second that," I said quickly, glancing around to make sure no one heard.

Dad was busy talking with James while Mom was busy impressing his mom, leaving Connor to get wasted, which, to be honest, wasn't like him at all. Something was troubling him, but we couldn't get into it now.

"Puh-leeze, give me a break," he slurred. His voice was louder and caught the attention of the table.

I stared at Barrett. "Come on, Connor, I think we can call it a night, huh?"

Connor got up. "Lovely to have met you!" He cheered the governor and his glamorous wife.

Dad and Mom looked mortified.

"I'll make sure he gets home," Barrett assured them.

No. I didn't want Barrett to go. Not yet. Not until… *what?* Maybe I'd pushed him away further tonight. Maybe he realized I wasn't what he wanted.

Everyone said their goodbyes to Barrett and Connor.

When it was my turn, he kissed me on the cheek dangerously close to my lips. I could almost feel them brush mine. I felt weak at the knees. His hand circled my hip, squeezing it. "Meet me in the library in five minutes," he whispered, his voice like a drug. I swallowed as I tried to compose myself.

"Nice to meet you, Barrett." Finigan held out his hand,

and Barrett shook it. I noticed a slight vein twitch in the side of Barrett's neck. "Likewise." His smile appeared genuine, but his cold eyes told otherwise.

After picking at my empty plate for five minutes and half-listening to Finigan, I excused myself from the table and set about for the library at the other end of the penthouse with my heart in my mouth. I walked into the dimly lit room. From nowhere, Barrett's hand grabbed mine, pulling me into the corner behind the door.

"Barrett!" I gasped. "Where's Connor?"

"Halfway home." He pressed his body close to mine, his warmth radiating up my bare arms.

His index finger traced the outline of my cheek, landing on my bottom lip. I sucked in a breath. "You're driving me fucking crazy, Lourde."

"Because you want me, Barrett."

He blinked, and I swallowed down my fear. His eyes darkened with a desperation I craved more than my freedom to be free from the binds of a Diamond heiress.

"Finigan won't ever be able to fuck you like I can." He breathed in my ear, and my pulse flew north.

"Maybe. Maybe not, but I bet he's capable of love."

He pressed me further into the wall, his body against mine." Is that what you really want?" he asked while his hands dug up under my dress. Throwing aside the designer dress like it was trash, he felt me through my lace panties.

"Yes," I whispered, unable to resist his hands on me.

He groaned. "Are you sure you don't just want this?"

He dipped his finger inside my folds. I was so wet for him.

Two fingers.

I threw my head back as a moan slipped from my lips.

"Shh, dollface. You don't want to get caught, now do you?"

"Barrett." My hands pulled the base of his hair as I felt his dick swell against my thigh. "We can't." I breathed out, trying to shake the feeling. "I deserve more than this," I said, somehow finding the strength to push him back.

Instantly, his hands were off me. I pulled my dress down while trying to catch my breath.

"I know you do."

"You do?"

He dragged his hands through his hair as his words hung in the air.

"Will you come to the house after? I think we should talk."

"Why?" I asked breathlessly.

"Just please tell me you will." There was a pleading in his eyes that hit me in the chest.

I shook my head. "I can't give you any promises, Barrett." I pushed off the wall and quickly brushed past him and out of the library toward the dining room.

"There you are." Finigan smiled, his blue eyes wide, his sandy hair perfectly parted to the side, dusting the tops of his ears.

"I'm here." I smiled.

"You looked flushed. Are you okay?"

Shit.

"Just tired is all."

"Well, we won't keep you any longer. Mom and Dad are ready to leave anyway. It was so nice to meet you, Lourde."

"You, too, Finigan."

"We can pretend that our parents haven't tried to set us up, but really, we're not idiots."

I laughed.

"To be honest, I'm thanking them for it." He gave me a bone-melting smile.

"You are?" I was honestly surprised by his admission.

He nodded. "I am."

He kissed me on the cheek, and I swear he could smell Barrett on me. I was going straight to hell.

"You okay?"

"Fine, yes," I stammered.

"So, will I see you again?"

"Sure."

He laughed. "Okay, Lourde. Ball's in your court. You've got my number."

"Sorry, I'm just—"

He put his hand up. "No need to say anything. I really enjoyed your company, and I think you're a beautiful woman."

Oh.

Before I could respond, his mother walked toward me and hugged me. "Lourde, lovely to have met you. I think Finigan is very fond of you, dear," she whispered in my ear.

I smiled. "Nice to meet you, Mrs. Connolly. Enjoy your vacation in Cannes."

After seeing them out, we finally retreated to the living room. I sat contemplating Barrett's request and the look in his eyes that called me.

Mom joined me while Dad poured himself a whiskey at the bar nearby.

"Well, that was a roaring success," Mom said.

"Except for our son getting blind drunk at the table," Dad interjected, sitting in his armchair.

"Well, yes, there was that minor mishap, but thank God for Barrett," Mom said, her gaze falling to me.

Thank God for Barrett indeed.

"So?" Mom inquired, her eyes wide.

"So?" I stared back.

"What did you think of Finigan?"

Oh, him.

"He's actually nice, Mom," I said, honestly.

"See!" She clapped her hands together.

Dad sat down, looking more tired than usual, and stared at mother. "You realize Lourde isn't your pet project."

She whipped her hand around. "Of course, I know that."

"Then maybe let her choose what she wants for a change."

Mom crossed her arms.

"Where has this come from?" she asked, exasperation in her tone.

Ignoring Mom, Dad turned to me. "Lourde, do you really want to work?"

"What?" Mom and I said at the same time, the water tumbler nearly falling from my hand.

"Of course, I do, Dad. I'd just given up asking."

"No, Lourde. I don't understand it. We women, we don't work," Mom argued.

"Liz!" Dad's tone was harsh, shooting her a steely glance.

"Mom, that's so old-fashioned and antiquated!" I was unable to stay silent any longer, knowing Dad might be on my side.

"I don't think it's a bad idea, Lourde." Dad smiled and threw me a wink.

I heard Mom sigh.

"Are you serious, Dad?"

"As a snake."

"I can't hear any more of this nonsense. I'm off to bed." Mom rose and excused herself from the room, muttering something under her breath.

"Don't worry about her. She'll get over it." Dad smiled.

"What brought this on, Dad?" I asked, shaking my head and closing my eyes at the realization I could actually do something with my life.

"Barrett, actually."

"Barrett?" I straightened in my seat.

"Yes. I was talking to him earlier about your time in the Hamptons, and he said you expressed concern of feeling trapped." He rubbed his temples in a brief show of vulnerability I hadn't seen from Dad before. "Anyway, if working frees you from that feeling, then I'm all for it, Lourde."

I leaped out of my seat and kissed him on the cheek. "Thank you! Thank you! Thank you!"

He laughed. "Any ideas what you want to do?"

"I might have a few." I smiled at the endless possibilities that lay ahead of me and all because of Barrett Black.

"I've just got to pop out, Dad."

He looked at his watch. "It's after eleven."

"I know." I ran my hand through my hair, toying with the ends.

"Why do I get the feeling I know where you're going."

I paused. Out of everyone, Dad could read me the best.

"I don't know what you're talking about," I said.

"Mm-hmm."

I cracked a smile before heading toward the door.

* * *

I'd only been to Barrett's a handful of times over the years, and that was because I was with Connor at the time when he was passing through. Each time, I'd always remained out front, though, never going inside.

With my heart in my throat, I ascended in the elevator,

unsure why I was even here. The soft background music was doing nothing to quell my nerves. The ping of the doors opening pulled me back to the present, and I stepped out just before they closed on me.

Minimal and not at all like his place in the Hamptons, the apartment was sleek, neutral, and modern. If his homes represented him, this place was the exterior he projected, whereas the Hamptons were the glimpses underneath he'd shown me during our time together.

"You came." He walked up to me barefoot and shirtless, every woman's wet dream. But his riptide of muscles and his dirty words couldn't distract me from what I truly deserved.

I needed to be strong.

27

BARRETT

The concierge buzzed, alerting me that Lourde had just arrived.

I found myself pacing the entire length of the apartment, anticipating this very moment.

"I'm here, Barrett," she said, wearing exactly the same outfit I'd seen her in an hour earlier.

"Thank you for coming." I scratched the crown of my head. "Come in, please." Awkward as fuck, I leaned in and kissed her on the cheek. Stepping back, I swallowed and turned, leading her into the living room. "What can I get you?"

Moving toward the kitchen, I fetched two glasses of water. "Wine? Coffee?"

"It's after midnight, Barrett. I shouldn't be here. I should be asleep."

Okay, I deserved that. I walked toward her, and she took a step back.

"But you're not. You're here."

"Yes, well, I wanted to thank you."

"For what?" She took the glass of water I handed her

and gestured toward the sofa. She walked over, taking a seat at the edge of the couch.

"You spoke to my dad about me wanting to work."

"He told you that?"

"Yes, after dinner tonight. He sat down with Mom and me."

"And?" I took a seat beside her.

"And I told him I want to work. He actually thinks it might be a good idea."

"That's amazing, Lourde. Did your mother flip?"

"She had already walked out by that point."

I laughed. "I bet."

She pushed a lock of hair away from her face, sliding it behind her ear. "So yeah, thanks, I guess."

"Pleasure, Lourde." I held her gaze before she pulled away.

"What will you do?" I asked.

"I don't know."

"We could use some help around ZF constructions now we've secured a new hotel. I know the boss, he's an asshole, but I could put in a good word for you." I tossed her a wink and a smile.

"I don't think that's a good idea, Barrett." She peered up from underneath her lashes.

Leaning forward, I tilted my head closer to hers.

Enough chit-chat.

I called her here for a reason. I sucked in a breath, my lungs pinching inward.

I took the water glass from her hand and put it on the coffee table, my thumb grazing her fingers. She dragged her teeth across her bottom lip at the connection.

"I think you should consider it. Not just because you're intelligent but because I don't think I can be apart from you."

"Wait, what?" A blush spread up her neck to her cheeks.

"I don't know if I can give you what you want, Lourde. Heck knows I don't deserve you, but with everything I am and everything I have, I'm willing to try."

She sat there, frozen. "Say something, please."

"In a world where it is without you, Barrett, or this, I choose whatever this is a million times over." Her lips tipped into a smile.

I pulled her onto my lap, her head an inch away from mine.

"And I'd rather die than have to watch you with another man again."

She laughed, placing her hands around my neck. "Sorry you had to sit through that."

"Fuck, so am I."

"And Connor?" she asked, her focus drifting down to my mouth.

"We'll figure it out with Connor," I said.

"What does that mean?"

"It means I don't give a fuck about anyone else but you. They can all perish under a cinder of smoke and ash."

"That might be just the most disturbing yet romantic thing you've ever said to me."

"And you love it, dollface."

"I do."

I pressed my mouth to hers. Lourde opened her soft lips and wrapped her hands around the nape of my neck. Her wet and warm tongue traced my lips. The glow of fireworks erupted inside of me.

The buzzer rang, interrupting our moment of pure bliss.

"Are you expecting someone?" she asked, arching an eyebrow and hopping off my lap.

"Hell, no." I walked over and held down the buzzer. "Yes."

"Mr. Black, I'm sorry to disturb you, sir, but I have Detective Summers here with his partner, Detective Davis. They say it's urgent."

"What the fuck? Now?"

"Afraid so, sir."

"All right, send them up."

"Is everything okay?"

"I have no idea, but it can't be good. It's after midnight, and detectives are on their way up here."

"Should I make myself scarce?" she asked.

Fuck, she had a point. She'd be recognized instantly, but I didn't care. I'd made up my mind, and I wanted Lourde, all of her. My chips were all in.

I held out my hand. "I want you beside me, Lourde, that's if you're willing to show the world you're mine."

"I've only ever been yours, Barrett," she said, taking her hand in mine.

THE END FOR NOW.

WANT MORE?

Want more of Lourde and Barrett sizzling romance?
Visit the link below for a scorching bonus scene…

https://dl.bookfunnel.com/yokgydxzyp

Or roll straight into the conclusion of Barrett in Lourde in Forbidden Love available here.

SLATER SIBLINGS SERIES

Hungry Heart

Chained Heart

Iron Heart

ELITE MEN OF MANHATTAN SERIES

Forbidden Lust*

Forbidden Love*

Lost Love

Missing Love

Guarded Love

SMALL TOWN DESIRES SERIES

Trusting the Rockstar

Trusting the Ex

Trusting the Player

*Forbidden Lust/Love are a duet and to be read in order. All other books are stand alones.

Join Missy's Club

Hear about exclusive book releases, teasers, discounts and book bundles before anyone else.

Sign up to Missy's newsletter here:
www.authormissywalker.com

Become part of Missy's Private Facebook Group where we chat all things books, releases and of course fun giveaways!

https://www.facebook.com/groups/
missywalkersbookbabes

ACKNOWLEDGMENTS

Many people support me, way too many to mention here. But an honorary mention goes to Alana.

2021 saw me grow in different ways as a writer and a human being. In some ways, it was my hardest year, but in others it was extraordinary.

Alana, you've pushed me beyond the limits I thought I could handle. You've shaken me up, rattled me and spun me around on a tumultuous rinse cycle. And for that, I thank you.

You are a unique and dear person, supporting me more than you'll ever know.

ABOUT THE AUTHOR

Missy is an Australian author who writes kissing books with equal parts angst and steam. Stories about billionaires, forbidden romance, and second chances roll around in her mind probably more than they ought to.

When she's not writing, she's taking care of her two daughters and doting husband and conjuring up her next saucy plot.

Inspired by the acreage she lives on, Missy regularly distracts herself by visiting her orchard, baking naughty but delicious foods, and socialising with her girl squad.

Then there's her overweight cat—Charlie, chickens, and border collie dog—Benji if she needed another excuse to pass the time.

If you like Missy Walker's books, consider leaving a review and following her here:

instagram.com/missywalkerauthor
facebook.com/AuthorMissyWalker
tiktok.com/@authormissywalker
amazon.com.au/Missy-Walker
bookbub.com/profile/missy-walker

Printed in France by Amazon
Brétigny-sur-Orge, FR